MW01124148

TUNNELS,
CAPPUCCINO,
AND A HEIST

MICHELE BONNELL

Copyright © 2013 by Michele Bonnell
All rights reserved
ISBN: 0988514826
ISBN 978-0-9885148-2-9
Library of Congress Control Number: 2012924174

This book is a work of fiction. The characters, names, incidents,
dialogue, events, businesses, organizations, are drawn from the
author's imagination or used fictitiously. Any resemblance to actual
events, locales, or persons, living or dead, is entirely coincidental.

Reading group guide copyright © 2012 by Blue Horizons
Publishing House
All rights reserved.

Printed in the United States of America. No part of this book may
be used or reproduced in any manner whatsoever without written
permission except in the case of brief quotations embodied in
critical articles and reviews.

FIRST EDITION
Library of Congress Cataloging-in-Publication Data

Blue Horizons Publishing House
St. Louis, Missouri, United States of America

Cover design by Larry Torno

For information www.michelebonnell.com

Blue Horizons
Publishing House

For keeping the dream real ...
John and Barbara Lutz

For keeping the dream real ...
John and Barbara Lutz

TUNNELS, CAPPUCCINO, AND A HEIST

PROLOGUE

*C*rime in the Central West End, a trendy neighborhood
of St. Louis that cocooned Forest Park, was a constant
... vandalism, auto theft, assaults, and an occasional
body found in the deep recesses of the sprawling park's thickly
wooded enclaves. The most recent crime was an afternoon
armed burglary along Maryland Avenue's upscale shops and
turn-of-the-century mansions. Four men in hoodies and masks
in a "smash and grab" shattered glass front windows of a retail
store for designer jeans, and cash of course.

But nestled nearby in Forest Park inside the guarded pristine
walls of the Art Museum that entombed millions of dollars worth
of art – Monet, Picasso, Van Gogh, Rembrandt – the attendees of
the fundraising event for the new Egyptian Wing felt quite safe.

No one expected what had been promoted as an exclusive mixer to end with the sound of sirens and suspicions.

They were waiting for the first unveiling of the infamous Egyptian faience - rumored to have been sold through an unscrupulous French-Lebanese dealer to the Art Museum.

The
DEBACLE

ONE

*T*he Museum was in an awkward position. By keeping the faience they would appear unethical. But to repatriate this once-in-a-lifetime art acquisition that could bring busloads of visitors to the Museum and generate untold amounts of new donors ... would be painful. And would no doubt result in some heads rolling at the top levels.

General sentiment, had a poll been taken, was that eventually the negative media would die down, Egypt's head of antiquities would return to Cairo, and St. Louis would enjoy her treasure.

But treasures sometimes have a higher price than their acquisition cost.

When Olivia read the brief story in the community section of the *St. Louis Sun Journal*, she had no idea that soon she would be at an exclusive mixer that ended with a chalk outline of a dead body.

On impulse she picked up the local paper, along with her usual handful of graphic design magazines, at the wedge of a retail store that sold newspapers and magazines. She was set for her Saturday ritual – a cappuccino, accompanied by perusing design magazines, and a jog through Forest Park.

Olivia flipped through the newspaper like a kid eating broccoli to get to the chocolate cake. Her eyes froze on a headline, "Egypt Demands Antiquity Return."

She folded the paper down the center and then in half for a deeper re-read. Egypt's head of antiquities claimed that the Art Museum had a stolen ceramic bowl that belonged in Cairo. He was calling for international media attention to investigate.

Olivia was distracted momentarily by an international story of such cultural significance tucked away in the newspaper's community section, but continued reading.

Dr. Hasaneen asserted that the bowl had vanished from a storage facility at an excavation site near Cairo. The more than three-thousand-year-old Egyptian faience was discovered missing when the antiquities were prepared for their trip to the Cairo museum. A global search located a photo of the bowl on the St. Louis Museum's website. The faience was the crowning jewel of a new Egyptian exhibit sponsored by St. Louis old and prestigious money - the Wentworth Foundation.

Ripping the story from the paper, Olivia secured it from the breeze by slipping it under her stack of magazines. Maybe she would stop by the Museum and take a look at this infamous faience.

Now for the chocolate cake. Sipping her foamy cappuccino, she spread out the magazines on the sidewalk table shaded by the pruned trees in one of St. Louis' trendy neighborhoods. The Central West End wrapped around Forest Park, one of the biggest city parks in the nation. It was notorious for zealous athletes, community events, museums, and crime.

"Olivia, did I just see you reading a print newspaper?"

She gazed up into her ex-fiancé's face and quickly straightened her hair and crossed her legs.

When they first met seven years ago, she was a voluptuous art school graduate who had just moved to New York City to pursue her art career dreams. Miles, an up and coming assistant curator, quickly swept her off her feet after they met at a lecture at The Metropolitan Museum of Art.

They lived together in Greenwich Village, she falling deeply in love and he falling deeply in infatuation.

She realized now that their engagement was simply a carrot to keep the relationship going. The actual karat never made it to her ring finger.

After two years of struggling to get her ceramic work shown in the competitive New York market, one of Miles' connections had booked one unsuccessful show.

So when Miles was offered a curator position at the Art Museum in St. Louis, she found a graphic design position at an agency and packed her bags to move back to her hometown. Six months later he split up with her.

And their careers in the art world had taken two distinctly different roads. Her art career was on hold from the creative drain of working at the advertising and public relations agency. His career was taking off as a noted chief curator in the art museum world with blogs and reviews speculating about his next move to the Smithsonian.

If she didn't still love him, she'd loathe him for having the life she wanted.

"Miles, are you spying on me?" His black-rimmed glasses brushed her cheek as she leaned toward his gentle kiss.

"You know it, sweet pea." This little southern nickname would have annoyed her coming from anyone else. But the contradiction from this transplanted New Yorker humored her.

"What's this?" He extracted the ripped newspaper page from the graphic design magazines. "It's in the local paper already?"

"Buried in the Community News section."

Miles laughed. "At least the paper is being gentle about it. Only in St. Louis, bless her heart." He loved this quirky town. She'd been good to him.

"Do you know anything about this Miles?" Olivia leaned in conspiratorially as he helped himself to a chair beside her.

"Of course."

"Tease. Spill it!"

"Without so much as a dinner?" he smiled coyly knowing exactly how to hit her buttons. Chemistry is an interesting thing. Try to turn it on and you can't, but try to turn it off when you need to leave well enough alone and …

"Fine, next dinner is my treat."

"This is actually really delicate Olivia. You know I'd trust you with my life, but I'd be in really hot water if the Museum found out."

"Wow! I've never seen you so secretive. " Olivia paused. Leaning in closer to him her dark hair spilled across his arm. "So what's it gonna take…"

When he didn't laugh, she pulled away from him and sat yoga straight. "You're serious."

"Olivia I know we're sitting at a little coffee shop in the Midwest. But this is an international debacle."

"Is the Museum in trouble?"

"Possibly."

"Juicy!!"

"Shame on you Olivia. That's my career."

Olivia wasn't sure if he was testy because she had managed to ignore his flirtations with her or if he was really that worried.

Answering his phone on the first ring, Miles crossed his legs and spoke like he was being charged by the word. Olivia pretended to not be listening to the series of uh-hums.

"Sweet pea, I have to go. There's an emergency meeting at the Museum. Apparently the Board has gotten wind about this media story. " He gave her a quick kiss and disappeared into the stream of pedestrians without divulging even a single word about the international debacle.

So, it was going to cost her a dinner.

TWO

The restaurant was one of the few places in St. Louis where you could get decent seafood. During the day it was full of high energy suits intent on their power meetings. At night it transitioned to romantic dinners, upscale family gatherings, and a smattering of West County physicians' wives out for a reserved girls' night.

Miles was always cheerful about a seafood dinner. And she wanted him in a receptive mood.

He arrived before her and had the telltale crumbs of one of their notorious biscuits remaining on the small white plate. "Sorry to start without you, sweet pea. Couldn't resist these biscuits."

"You have amazing genes. I'd be huge if I tried to keep up with you."

She lifted her sunglasses and situated them atop her head. Miles observed her. "What?"

"You just have the most remarkable green eyes."

"You're such a flirt. Don't temp me. You know it's been awhile since I've dated what's-his-name."

"Oh yes, that engineer guy? Let's not discuss. Time to look at the menu before our appetites go away." He scanned the over-sized menu. "They have your favorite rainbow trout today."

"Wonderful! I'm starving." The traffic had been heavy for a Tuesday afternoon. One of the major highways that dissected the city was in the midst of a three-year construction project. And trying to get out of the agency early was tricky. She had two annual reports to design for clients before Friday in addition to preparing the graphics for a client presentation for the pitch team.

A waiter stopped by. Miles dotingly ordered the rainbow trout for her. He straightened his crisp blue shirt that contrasted elegantly with his perfectly groomed black hair, and smiled.

She fussed with her silverware and napkin as she considered ways to get Miles to tell all about the Museum debacle. Miles gingerly consumed yet another biscuit. What a chess player. He had to know she was absolutely bursting with curiosity.

"Stop being coy! You know what I want to know!" The perfectly placed knife clattered to the floor as her hand came down emphatically on the table. She sighed as a few nosey restaurant guests glanced their way.

He looked amused at her display. "Olivia, you're all wound up. Are they overworking you again at that heartless agency?"

"I'm just wanting a tiny little morsel of information about the Egyptian story. Is that too much to ask after all our years together?"

"Excellent application of guilt. My mother would be proud." Miles straightened his napkin across his lap before he appraised her for a few moments. She managed to hold her ground and say nothing. "Alright sweet pea. But this has to stay between you and me. And if you ever leak a word, I don't know you."

"Agreed."

"Egyptian antiquities are the most sought after pieces for museums. Their history and allure bring in visitors and more importantly deep pocket benefactors. It's highly competitive to get these pieces. And a real coup for any museum director. Sometimes these antiquities come into the art world in unusual ways. Let's just say they cross a few bridges if you know what I mean."

She wasn't sure if she understood, but she didn't want to slow him down by asking.

"It's a raging debate in the world of high art. Do you accept these pieces that may not come through the right channels? If you pass on them, another museum or collector will not resist them. Then your museum has lost the game. "

"Miles, are you saying that it's common for disreputable people to sell Egyptian antiquities?" Olivia thought that a renowned museum wouldn't want to risk their reputation for one piece of art.

He raised his brows at her naiveté just as their salads were placed before them. Pausing, he watched as the waiter moved to another table and out of eavesdropping range. "I'm afraid so, sweet pea." He crunched on a few bites of crisp salad. "Not that I agree with this. But I have to say I see both sides."

"Both sides?"

"Well of course Egypt has every right to insist upon the legitimate purchase and transfer of antiquities from their country. But if they cannot control these pieces from escaping out of Egypt, then the chances of their return are extremely slim."

"That's awful! You can't condone that black market conduct. Has working in a museum so long brainwashed you?" He looked surprised by her outburst. "Art belongs to the country of origin unless it's rightfully purchased. I simply can't see both sides."

He listened to her quietly, finished his salad, and then crossed his long lean legs. "You haven't taken a bite of your salad Olivia."

"I find this upsetting. Perhaps I'll never be a real artist, but I have complete respect for how art is treated. And this complacency about what amounts to smuggling artifacts is just wrong."

"I understand your point. Just keep in mind that there is another side."

They sat in uncomfortable silence during the main course. Finally, Miles broke the silence, "I admire your passion Olivia. Can we call a truce?"

She sighed. Miles was too good of a friend for this tension. And he had just risked his career to give her some of the juicy story she had begged for. "Yes, of course. How's your salmon?"

He smiled, "Exceptional. Are you up for dessert?"

Olivia laughed, "Where does it all go? I'll have a cappuccino while you have dessert."

Driving home from the restaurant, she rewound their conversation in her mind. It struck her so hard she almost hit her brakes. Miles was the Museum's curator. He knew how driven the Museum's director was. He knew that the Museum needed an attention-grabbing acquisition to gain recognition in the museum world.

Could her ex-fiancé be involved in this international debacle?

THREE

The Art Museum was pleasantly cool after her brief Saturday jog. She started her jog late after digging through websites about Egyptian antiquities. By mid-morning the humidity was so dense she felt like she had jogged through a pool rather than Forest Park.

Sprinkles of museum visitors wandered about. A couple debated as they pointed at their museum map. They sauntered toward the East wing but then turned in front of her and headed toward the West Wing. The salt-and-pepper-haired man turned toward her offering an apologetic smile before they disappeared into the corridor.

At the information desk a white-haired woman provided lengthy answers to a tangle of questions from an inquisitive visitor. Olivia waited. Nearly five minutes later she wondered why only one person was working at an information center on a Saturday. She presumed this was a busy day for them. She repositioned her stance for the continued wait. Patience did not come naturally to her.

Another five minutes passed. She allowed herself a prompting sigh. Finally the white-haired woman with the unrelenting information looked her direction. "We'll be with you in just a moment."

She didn't understand the need for saying we. But at least she had gotten some attention. One step closer to getting her information.

Finally the guy in front of her seemed satiated by the nearly fifteen minutes of discussion and muttered a few words before moving on. Olivia smiled at the woman. "Good morning."

"Good afternoon. What may I help you with?"

Olivia noticed the clock behind the woman had drifted to past noon. She must have an internal clock.

"Yes, I'm interested in seeing the Egyptian faience recently acquired by the museum."

Without blinking she replied, "I'm not familiar with the piece."

Olivia paused. She hadn't expected a complete dismissal.

"Certainly you must be. It's been promoted on your website for the new Egyptian Exhibit."

"Sorry, I don't know where it would be."

The pleasantly cool air in the Museum had suddenly become chilly.

Like poker players bidding on a high stakes pot, they eyed each other.

"Ma'am, there's even been an article in the newspaper about the piece. Anyone here should be familiar with it."

"I'm sorry, but I don't have any information for you. Is there anything else I can help you with?"

Clearly there was no way around this programmed speech. "No." Olivia headed toward the West Wing. Twenty-foot vertical panels with mummy graphics book-ended the new Egyptian Exhibit.

As Olivia entered the Exhibit, she glanced back at the information desk. The austere volunteer was on the phone speaking in a flurry as she slid a reproachful look toward her.

Olivia felt like a tagged animal caught by a team of statistical zealots.

A simple question about the faience had marked her already.

The vibration of her Blackberry startled her. Not because she wasn't accustomed to it interrupting her weekends. The agency was in a constant state of project triage. The competition for clients was so vicious that impossible deadlines were an accepted way of life. Having a life outside of the agency, to create art or even date, was a challenge.

Jonathon, a conservator who worked with Miles at the Museum, rigorously contested that her graphic design career at the agency blocked her from her dream of becoming an artist. The sixty-hour work weeks and creative drain made it impossible to have any energy to create high art he argued.

"Be a waitress, work at Starbucks, whatever will pay for a cheap apartment," he persuaded, "But get away from that agency. It's a creative carnivore."

Sometimes she thought about it. But starving for high art and living in a moldy cheap apartment just didn't sound inspiring to her. Besides, she had allergies.

There was really no end to her excuses to avoid the true test of her creative abilities.

Maybe her dream of being an artist was simply that, a dream.

For today, her mission was to find that faience. After dealing with the austere volunteer, she was determined to find this notorious ceramic bowl that had inspired complaints from Egypt's head of antiquities.

Beyond the tall vertical banners, Olivia entered into the new Egyptian exhibit through a tunnel-shaped portal made of faux limestone. Passing through the tunnel wide enough across for six people and nearly two stories tall, she entered into a cool chamber with darkened windows. The exhibit pieces were no longer in glass cases, but positioned in cavernous displays along the composite stonewalls. Graphics of hieroglyphics were interspersed along the walls. In the center of the room was a round kiva-shaped display, the main attraction.

Olivia took a minute to soak it all in. The Museum had invested considerably in the tomb-like exhibit.

Two women ahead of her peaked into the kiva and quickly moved on to a display along the wall.

How indifferent, she thought. Society could be so unappreciative of art. From the dismissal of art classes at many public schools to the inadequate support of new artists, the lack of artistic understanding was dismal.

She walked respectfully forward to the kiva. The center of attention in this elaborate, and clearly expensive, exhibit was due considerable time and reflection.

Peering into the glass-topped kiva, she observed a flat platform spread with river rock with a center square of flagstone. An empty square.

Where was the artifact?

She stepped back to read the display signage – Egyptian Faience dedicated by the Wentworth Foundation.

"Pardon me, ma'am."

A museum guard, a young woman with an employee badge, and a man with a tool belt greeted her as she turned around. She moved aside as they formed a semi-circle around the exhibit and the man with the tool belt detached the display signage from the exhibit. They left without discussion.

The exhibit attending guard remained in the room staring casually ahead at a self-imposed mark on the wall.

"Sir, do you know if they've moved the Egyptian faience? I'd very much enjoy seeing it." Olivia smiled sweetly.

"I don't have any idea, ma'am." The guard continued staring at the wall.

"Whom could I check with to find out?"

"The Information Desk would be your best bet."

Right.

The Blackberry vibrated again. She checked the text message. Another SOS for her to come into the office. Another Saturday afternoon at the agency. Maybe working at Starbucks wouldn't be a bad idea.

After she texted the office to let them know she was on her way, she called her friend Jonathon.

"Liv! What happened to my cappuccino buddy?"

"I know, I know. It's been relentless at the agency. But I really want to catch up. "

"Are you sure? I was afraid I'd lost you to Miles."

"Don't be silly Jonathon. I'm not going back to Miles."

"Deal. Cappuccino this evening?"

"It's in the Blackberry."

Olivia ended the call feeling a little guilty. She intended to take a little advantage of their friendship and pump him for information about the faience.

She'd definitely have to buy his cappuccino. And a pastry.

FOUR

It was a typical summer day in St. Louis – ninety-something degrees with humidity that rivaled a wet sauna. Her aging Nissan was an omelet on the blacktop parking lot of the agency. Opening the passenger door first then the driver's door, she leaned into the oppressive heat of the interior to start the ignition and open the sunroof. After waiting thirty seconds, she circled round to close the passenger door and returned to her side settling into the scalding leather seat. She was counting the days to fall.

AC turned full blast; she headed to the coffee shop to meet Jonathon. He was waiting for her at a table outside the coffee shop.

"Hey Jonathon. Let's get a table inside today ok?"

Wearing shorts and a t-shirt, he wrinkled his nose in disinterest. He was cold-blooded having been raised in the open-window culture of France. Jonathon had acclimated to American culture and lifestyle in all ways except for this annoyance with AC. The excessive use of refrigerated air never made sense to him.

"Sorry, but my laundry time was taken over by another Saturday at the agency. These jeans will stick to me like glue out here in the sun."

"I have an extra pair of shorts in my bag."

"Yuck. No thanks." She tugged at his arm in encouragement until he reluctantly entered the AC interior.

"Let me get the cappuccinos." Olivia coaxed. "And pick a pastry de jour."

"Wow, what's the occasion? Liv, are you up to something?"

"Can't a friend treat a friend without some intent behind it?"

He cocked his head, contemplating. "Hmmm. No."

She laughed and bumped shoulders with him. "Don't spoil my treat."

But Jonathon knew her too well. They had met five years ago, shortly after she returned to St. Louis, at a gallery walk. She was eavesdropping on his discussion about the nude model in an open-to-the-public gallery setting. Two artists debated that it was a realistic view of the art world and methods. Jonathon felt that it was too much for the general public. Olivia chimed in that it was unfair to expose the model to a general audience. The group burst into laughter at her use of "expose." Jonathon came to her rescue and introduced himself. As the years passed, he started referring to her as Liv, the name her family used most often, and became the brother she'd always wanted.

"I was going to get a frappuccino, but in here a cappuccino will be better." He scoured the pastries before selecting a cherry tort.

They grabbed a table for two near the window.

"How's the pastry?"

"Wonderful. Thanks for the treat." Jonathon corralled a few dropped crumbs into a tidy circle and swept them onto the plate he lowered to table level. "Is this a sympathy treat because of the big argument between Miles and me?"

"Well maybe." She felt a needle of guilt for the small lie and moved on quickly. "We had lunch at his favorite seafood restaurant …?

"It's been a bit tense at the Museum. I'm sure you've read about the repatriation situation and the Egyptian head of antiquities requesting our newly acquired faience back."

Olivia shifted in her seat and tried not to look too anxious. Was it possible that their argument was about the Egyptian artifact? She nodded and sipped her cappuccino, her eyes encouraging him to continue.

"Well Miles and I have two very different perspectives on the matter. And it's much more than my professional opinion as a conservator. We're debating this whole hot button issue of repatriation. And it's causing an uncomfortable civil war at the Museum. You might as well give us team numbers and jerseys."

"Jonathon that must be a political nightmare."

"Tell me about it. I'm on the opposite side of our chief curator."

"I'm so sorry Jonathon." She held his forearm for a minute.

"Thank you Liv." He sipped his coffee. "I mean people should be able to discuss differences and maintain civility. We're not corporate puppets. Opinions should be appreciated. Don't you think?"

"Yes, of course they should."

He shook his head and looked out at the busy sidewalk.

A few medical residents in scrubs passed by headed to nearby overpriced apartments within walking distance of Washington University School of Medicine. Backpacks weighing them down, they looked extraordinarily tired.

She wandered if the agency was doing the same to her.

"It was just a simple disagreement."

Good. He was going to open up without her probing. She gave him her full attention.

"Really I would say a difference of philosophical viewpoints. But Miles got stuck on 'the principle of the matter' and wouldn't let it go. So the argument just escalated and escalated. We were actually yelling at each other..."

"This was at the Museum?"

"At a staff meeting."

They were momentarily silenced by the whirling clatter of the frappuccino blender that could compete with a helicopter landing.

"You'd think they could find a quieter way to do that."

"I could deal with the blender if they'd just turn down this arctic AC," Jonathon said.

She rolled her eyes at him, "You and the AC nemesis. Let's get back to what happened with the big argument. What did you mean by philosophical difference?"

"Philosophical viewpoints," he corrected. "Miles believes it's ok for a museum to purchase art that was acquired through questionable resources. I completely, wholeheartedly, unequivocally disagree."

"Good for you Jonathon!"

He cocked an eyebrow.

"Seriously. I agree with you one hundred percent. No, one hundred and ten percent."

Grabbing her hand, he took a deep breath. "I love you kiddo."

She gave him her brightest smile, "Of course you do."

Jonathon and Olivia tightened their grips like a pre-game team rally and then released one another's hands.

He returned to his people watching. There was always something interesting to see in the Central West End, from college students to hip retirees.

"So do you think the faience should be returned to Cairo?" Olivia confirmed.

The sun broke from behind a gargoyle defending the century old office building across the street.

"Absolutely." His ocean blue eyes changed to steamy cobalt.

"Do you think the Museum will return it?"

"When the Mississippi turns into an ice-rink."

"That's what I thought."

"The new director is greedy. He'll do anything to pump up the Museum and his career." He chuckled quietly. "He told Miles that he had his sights on being a Smithsonian director."

"That's ambitious."

"He passed ambitious at the last block."

"No wonder Dr. Hasaneen is angry at him."

"What's this? Are you buddies with the media-savvy Egyptian head of antiquities?"

"Not exactly. I just read up on this a little." She sipped her cappuccino then stirred it around awhile. "I have a confession."

He looked at her expectantly. She paused. Why was she having a hard time telling him this?

"Liv, would it help if I was behind a curtain?"

"No, it's not that big. Ok. I went to the Art Museum to look at the artifact."

"Why is that a big confession? I'm sure other folks did the same thing after that article in the newspaper."

"I guess so. But it wasn't there. And the information volunteer pretended to know nothing about it."

"I'm not surprised. The Museum is waiting to unveil it at a big fundraiser. They may be evaluating that decision after the negative media."

"Well it gets stranger. More strange. Whichever. I was looking at the empty display when a trio of museum staff came round and removed the dedication plaque."

"Really?"

"Yes. And then they just left. No replacement plaque."

"Interesting." He rubbed his chin. "My guess is that our benefactor doesn't want to get mud on their name."

She nodded in agreement.

"Do you think that's why the photo was taken off the Museum's website also?"

He chuckled. "You have done your homework. Hmm. I think they may have taken it off the site to calm the media exposure."

"Do you have any literature on it?"

"If you want to see it, I can make arrangements."

"To see the artifact?"

"No, that's locked away. Just some pics."

She felt a rush of warmth as her face flushed with excitement.

"Liv, you're blushing. Are you falling under the spell of the magical faience?"

"The spell? What are you talking about?"

"I'll fill you in when I show you the pics. But our meters are probably expired. Let's head out before my cappuccino treat costs me a parking ticket."

FIVE

S unday morning was luxuriously quiet. Her apartment neighbors were a mix of young professionals
and medical residents. The young professionals
were sleeping it off after a late night of partying and the
residents had passed out from sleep deprivation.

When her Blackberry vibrated she groaned. If it was
the agency, she was seriously going to consider becoming
a starving artist and working at Starbucks. But the text
was from Jonathon – *Check out the Arts & Entertainment
Section of the St. Louis Sun Journal. Print version. Not on the
online version for some reason.*

So much for sleeping in.

Tossing on a ball cap and sunglasses, she wandered over to the local newsstand two blocks away. Omar was behind the counter as usual, working endless hours to bring his family here from Africa. He welcomed her warmly. How did he keep his outlook so positive living such a hard, lonely life? She always left the newsstand benefited by his ability to transfer happiness.

Back in her apartment, she spread the newspaper out on her unmade bed. Grabbing the Arts & Entertainment section, she spotted the story.

The headline - "Museum's New Artifact Linked to King Tut's Mother" - was on the section's first page in large print. The story was longer than the previous snippet buried in the Community Section. She read it twice before calling Jonathon.

"What took you so long to call?"

"Less than 30 minutes is a long time? I had to run over and get the paper after all."

"Oh yes. How's Omar?"

Everyone in the Central West End loved Omar.

"Cheerful as usual."

"Not getting the same from you, Miss Cranky."

"Sorry. I was trying to sleep in and still haven't woken up. Jonathon, is it true that the artifact could have belonged to King Tut's mother?"

"Well you certainly can't believe everything you read in The Sun. But I hear there may be some talk about this at the upcoming Museum fundraiser."

"Really? Who all is invited to this fundraiser?"

"Big donors, the Board, a few dignitaries, and a handful of academics."

"Will media be there?"

"My guess is that this event will be kept private."

"Why?"

"Word is that they plan to unveil the faience and schmooze it up with the benefactors."

"I want to come to the fundraiser."

"Good luck. It's a short list. Only the muckety-mucks."

"I see."

"Now Olivia don't get into an embarrassing situation. Security is going to be very tight. No walk-ins."

"Please. I'm more creative than that."

Jonathon laughed. "No doubt."

———

She approached her new challenge like a design project. First establish a theme and then a look. As a high-end donor, she needed to develop a persona – someone new to St. Louis. Someone that would make the Museum drool over attracting her as a benefactor. Maybe a Texas oil heiress? She'd screw up the accent. Something closer to her experience. After two years in New York, she could do a near perfect Upper East Side accent. Of course, daughter of a publishing tycoon and avid art collector. A little mysterious and certainly upscale.

Now for the look. A sophisticated, hip, cosmopolitan look would work well. Of course she had nothing like that to wear.

It was time to call in the troops. Her friend Lisa would know exactly which upscale second-hand stores to hit. And her husband was available to watch their kids today.

After a few hours digging through the jam-packed racks of five second-hand stores, they came up with the perfect outfit – black designer slacks, a sleek black cami, and a sassy black bolero punctuated by a red clutch, gold bangles, and shimmery gold dangle earrings.

Lisa admired the outfit in the chipped dressing room mirror. "My work here is done. Have fun on your hot date!"

Olivia thought it best to not mention the Museum to too many friends. "I will."

On Tuesday, she slipped out the back door of the agency for another rare out-of-the-office lunch. She had called the Museum fund development department the day before and, after sharing the construed profile of her faux affluent New York family, they eagerly arranged a lunch meeting at the Museum.

At the Museum, she parked in the back lot keeping the aging Nissan out of sight and avoiding the ever-so-observant Information Desk volunteer.

The restaurant's curved windows overlooked an isolated plaza speckled with pots of red gardenias and white hyacinth. A young staffer in a navy blue suit sat toward the back, a folder and pen positioned to the left of the table setting. She rose quickly when she saw Olivia and rushed across the room to greet her.

"Ms. Steinberg?" she bubbled.

"Yes it is," Olivia drew out the three words for emphasis lacing them with an aloof tone.

"I'm Rebecca Woods. We're so glad you came to see us today."

"Well my father very much appreciated the Arts."

Her real father actually did love the Arts. When she was sixteen, he disappeared to Greece and took all of his art pieces with him. Her Mom told her later that those pieces would be valued in the low six figures. But he had paid the child support and for Olivia's art degree at Washington University. A small purchase to appease his guilt for leaving his family and starting a new life with his mistress in Athens.

Rebecca started into a long explanation about the rich history of the Museum and some of their new exhibits. The waiter fussed over them bringing a decorative lunch followed by a coffee. She noticed that the other guests at the restaurant were receiving much less attention. Rebecca continued chattering about the new Egyptian exhibit for nearly ten minutes before Olivia interrupted.

"I do have some interest in this Egyptian exhibit. My earliest memories are of visiting the Cairo museum. My father was intrigued by the Egyptian art."

The young staffer kept the enthusiasm rolling, "How fascinating to have been to the Cairo museum."

"You haven't been?" Olivia raised her brows. She needed to get the upper hand here.

"No ma'am. But I hope to go soon."

"I see." She surveyed the room with bored disapproval. "Well I really must be going."

The young staffer nervously handed her the folder with the Museum literature. "We hope you'll join our Friends Club. The support of our Museum is so important to our community and the art world."

"I can certainly appreciate that. But I'm more accustomed to a more social role for benefactors."

"Certainly! Well, there is a benefactors event coming up for our Egyptian exhibit."

Bingo.

"Oh?"

"Yes, it's a short list. Very exclusive. But I think I can get you on the list."

"I would consider this invitation. Of course, I'll have to check my calendar."

"Of course, of course," the young staffer smiled sweetly.

"And what day is it?"

"Oh, yes," she giggled nervously. "It's this Saturday."

"Saturday? I'm booked already."

If there was one thing Olivia knew already from her dating life, it was to never act too available.

"Well, if you could move things around we'd just love to have you. I'll make sure you're on the list."

"I'll see what I can do."

———

Olivia realized she now had only a few days to find an outfit worthy of the daughter of a New York publishing tycoon. The second-hand shops wouldn't work for the discerning eyes of the benefactors crowd.

The next evening she found herself milling about the second floor of Saks like a pound puppy. The price tags nearly laughed at her when she tried to discreetly flip them over to "look for the right size." She'd never spent hundreds of dollars for one dress. Even though she was opposed to the idea, she entertained the thought of returning the carefully worn dress after the fundraiser. She could already hear the admonishment from her mother if she found out.

One hour later she left the store with a beautiful little black dress and a credit card in the red.

Her Blackberry vibrated – a text from Jonathon. *Stop by to see the pics!*

Be there in twenty minutes, she texted back.

Jonathon's apartment was just three blocks from her place, an easy walk. But it had started to rain. So she tested her luck and hunted for a parking spot by his place. She circled around twice before a space opened up. Her luck was good today.

She called his number on the security panel of the building door and he promptly buzzed her in. The lobby was an elegant art deco. Jonathon had good taste. Her apartment building was plain in comparison. It was also a couple hundred dollars less a month. The Museum was more generous with salary than her agency.

He'd left his apartment door ajar for her.

Jonathon was just setting down a couple glasses of wine on the mahogany coffee table stacked with books, brochures, and papers. She eyed the books and started getting that prickly feeling of excitement.

He chuckled, "Your eyes are lit up Liv. I'm going to have to keep an eye on you and this faience."

Sitting down beside him, she reached for one of the books.

He blocked her gently. "Hold on. Let me walk you through this." He handed her a glass of wine and assumed a docent role.

"The books are mainly reviewing the time period of the faience, the life of King Tut, and some background on the Egyptian faience. The faience is a nonclay ceramic or silica made from quartz, soda or lime, and ground copper and was used for beads, rings, figurines, and vessels to name a few. Although it's a nonclay material, it is fired and can be molded, carved, or inlaid…

Olivia settled in taking a sip of her wine.

"The ancient Egyptian word for faience, tjehnet, means dazzling because of its reflective qualities. The use of copper during firing produces a blue green color. Faience was associated with light. And faience vessels, considered to be magical, have been found in King Tut's treasures. Art historians believe that faience was passed on from earlier periods. The aquatic motifs on the vessels are usually a pool of water, plants, and fish. Some believe this symbolizes the waters of creation. Historians believe the motifs may have temple and funerary context. Either way, anyone who views the beauty of the turquoise faience is struck by the magnetic energy."

She listened to her friend and saw him in a new light. Not only was his knowledge impressive, but also his way of bringing the art to life was admirable.

"So we come to the faience of question. The faience in St. Louis. Now hidden from view…"

He pulled a portfolio out from the stack of books, opened it and selected a page with his forefinger and thumb. Delicately setting it on the table, he withdrew her glass of wine as she leaned in to see the photo.

She stared at the turquoise bowl unable to take her eyes away. The warm blue was the richest color she had seen. A lotus design etched in black filled the inside of the bowl while a few specks of colorless faience revealed the ancient texture. She felt her eyes watering from the pure beauty of the vessel.

Pulling herself away from the photo, she faced Jonathon. "The faience must be returned to Egypt."

"Agreed. But who could make this happen my friend?"

SIX

She hadn't slept well the rest of the week. The faience interrupted her sleep with strange dreams. And her days were distracted with thoughts of the haunting photo and the possibility that she might see the real thing at the fundraiser.

Determined to rest, she took a Tylenol PM and went to bed early on Friday. She needed her beauty sleep for her debut as the New York heiress tomorrow.

Sipping her second cup of coffee, she suddenly realized that her debut would be ruined if she was seen anywhere near her sun-faded Nissan. An heiress wouldn't be driving an eight-year-old car designed for the middle market.

She needed a limousine.

What was that going to cost?

Seven phone calls later she found a start up limo company that accepted her offer to provide a new, professionally designed logo for the car services.

The sleek black limo arrived promptly at six-thirty. The driver, impeccably dressed in black, opened her door with the finesse of a concert pianist.

Showtime.

The fundraiser started at six-thirty. She arrived fashionably late at six-forty five. Taking time to be seen, she stretched her toned legs out of the car and accepted the driver's hand for a perfect lift. Several groups walking up the stairs to the Museum entrance pivoted in reaction to the turned heads eyeing her. The driver stood by the car, providing her the royalty status of waiting for her full entrance before he returned to the air-conditioned interior.

The limo company was definitely going to get a fantastic logo.

Rebecca, the fund development staffer, greeted guests at the entrance.

"Ms. Steinberg! We're so glad you could make it!" She ushered her into the reception, assisting her with finding the hors d'oeuvres and introducing her to a few of the shortlist crowd. The event was staged in the mezzanine beside the tall panels of the Egyptian Exhibit entrance. Golden silk curtains hung across the entrance, blocking the view into the exhibit. It appeared that an unveiling was in order.

A small group gathered around her and bombarded her with questions. Being introduced as the daughter of a New York art connoisseur had resulted in a deluge of conversation. Which works did her father own? From which period? Was his collection significant?

Olivia spotted a tall-dark-and-handsome thirty something standing by himself near the table of desserts. "Pardon me, I see someone I know."

He looked startled when she walked directly toward him.

"Pretend you know me. You're saving me from a dreadfully boring conversation."

When he laughed his dark eyes looked even more magnetic. She'd have to be careful not to let this guy distract her.

"I'm happy to assist such a beautiful woman, Miss..."

His exotic accent brought the scent of jasmine to mind.

"Miss..uhm," she almost forgot her faux last name. "Miss Steinberg."

"So it is Miss?"

"Oh yes."

His smile made it a little hard to breath.

"My name is Amro." He started to put his hand out to shake hers.

She tisked at him and arched her eyebrows to the dull conversationalists. "Amro, we can't shake hands if we already know each other."

"Right. Sorry about that."

The clinking of a wine glass brought everyone's attention to the center of the room. The Museum director was ready to make an announcement.

"Welcome everyone to one of the most exciting receptions I've been privy to in my tenure at this wonderful Museum," he beamed. "I have an exceptional announcement to make to you, our very select group of Friends. And then you'll be the first to gaze upon a work of art so beautiful that it may change your life. To experience beauty of this level is beyond what many have in a lifetime. As a matter of fact, more than anyone has had in centuries. Our Egyptian faience, the exceptional gift of our benefactor, the Wentworth Foundation..." He paused to allow the group to applaud and the Wentworth's to drop a little nod of acknowledgement. "The faience will be unveiled in just a few minutes. But first, a momentous announcement. You are the first to officially know that this exquisite faience is accurately believed to belong to King Tut's mysterious mother. This is the first artifact to be discovered from King Tut's mother."

The crowd gasped and broke into heightened conversation with one another. The director clinked his wine glass again.

"If I may have your attention... We are finishing our transport of the faience as we speak. So if you would graciously excuse me, I'll check on its proper placement before inviting you into the Egyptian Exhibit to see a work of art that will haunt your dreams."

Olivia felt a little prickle at the recollection of the strange dreams she'd had since she saw the photos of the faience. Feeling suddenly thirsty, she realized her excitement level was elevated not only because of the handsome man beside her. The gravity of the faience, its history, and the significance of the finding had sunk in. This was an historical find. It really wasn't overstated to say it was an epic find.

She wondered why only a handful of museum guards were at the event. The artifact had to be worth millions.

After the Museum director had been gone a considerable amount of time the crowd started to get restless. Gazes diverted to the silky golden curtains at the entrance of the new Egyptian Wing. The hors d'oeuvres and wine dwindled.

An established-looking gentleman strolled over to Rebecca and leaned into a hushed conversation. She nodded and crossed the mezzanine, darting behind the curtains.

The scream shook the crowd. Glasses of wine slipped to the floor. A guard rushed through the curtains that slipped from the wire and dropped to the cold marble. The crowd inched forward.

The Museum director was on the floor, one leg crooked behind him and the other arm stretched the opposite direction. Rebecca stood beside him, holding her mouth to muffle the screams that were no longer auditory.

Three more guards swarmed into the exhibit. One directed Rebecca to stand by a wall, the second corralled the encroaching crowd away from the exhibit room, and the third discretely moved Olivia and Amro out of the mezzanine to the back entrance. To Olivia's great relief, the limo had parked in the back. She waved him over as the sirens of the surge of St. Louis police heightened.

The driver took the back road avoiding the wave of police cruisers descending on the Museum entrance. Olivia could see the flash of blue lights through the columns of dense trees.

She turned to Amro. He was staring straight ahead in a classic deer-caught-in-the-headlight mode.

"Would you like to get a cup of coffee?"

He looked at her as if he just realized she was sitting in the back seat with him. "What?"

"A cup of coffee."

"Oh."

Time to turn on some charm if she was going to figure out who this guy was. "Might as well. For some reason, I don't think we're going to sleep tonight anyhow."

The limo looked presumptuous double-parked at the neighborhood Starbucks. But having just crashed a high-end fundraiser, observed the likely murder of the Museum's director, and escaped out the back entrance with a stranger, this was the least of her concerns.

SEVEN

The coffee shop was unusually quiet. Amro looked around the room carefully. Perhaps checking to see if he knew anyone. Maybe a girlfriend?

He'd graciously bought her coffee, but ordered only tap water for himself. They sat along a wall away from the inhabited tables. She let a few minutes of awkward silence drift by while she collected her thoughts. He didn't seem to mind.

"So, Amro…"

His eyes lifted from their observance of the rim of his plastic cup. A little jolt of electricity ran through her.

This guy was trouble. The kind of trouble she could fall into like a luxurious feather mattress.

"So miss …" he smiled.

She returned the grin. "Quite an evening so far, wouldn't you say?"

"It's different from most of my evenings."

"Really? What are most of your evenings like?" She hadn't meant to insert the suggestiveness into the question. But the way his dark eyes were summing her up was bringing out her flirtatious side.

"Different," he shrugged.

So he liked to play his cards close to the cuff. She liked a challenge.

"So Amro do you know the guard that ushered us out the back door?"

"Yes."

She played the waiting game. The silence had no impact on his composure.

"Miss Steinberg, do you have a first name?"

"I do."

"Would you like to share it?"

"Sure." She waited for him to reel her in.

"With me?"

"Oh, yes." She grinned, enjoying the little game. "It's Olivia."

"Olivia…" he absorbed the information. "This name has meaning in my culture."

"How interesting. What culture is that?"

"Egyptian."

Now it was her turn to keep her composure. She was beginning to seriously wonder why this guy was at the exhibit the night the Museum director was murdered. And how did he know the guard?

"Egyptian? Wow, you're the first Egyptian I've met."

"That means we're linked then Olivia."

"Linked?"

"We have significance to each other."

"Well since we just rushed out the back door and disappeared from the scene of what appears to be the murder of the Museum director, I think you're right."

His laughter brought new energy to the quiet coffee shop. Was he trying to win her over? A simple phone call to the police sharing that an Egyptian at the scene of the crime knew the guard would get this guy a lot of questions. Of course, those questions would then turn to her since she had left with him and had established an alias for herself when attending the event.

He was right. They were linked.

"I consider it my good fortune to be linked with such a beautiful woman, Olivia."

If anyone else had said that, she would have thought it to be completely corny. His sensuality made it provocative. Falling into that feather bed was starting to tease her mind. And her body. How long had it been now since her breakup with the uptight engineer? Seven months, two weeks, and four days. Not that she was counting.

Her family loved him. He would offer stability and keep her structured. Marrying the engineer, one year shy of her thirtieth birthday, would finally get her off the market and allow her mother to focus on other things. Like a relentless pursuit for grandchildren.

She simply couldn't marry the non-stop linear methodologist that needed to measure everything. The last straw was what he considered an enlightened approach to sexual activity. A remedy for Olivia being tired after work.

Not having the heart to tell him that he was becoming less interesting in bed, she had listened to his diatribe about scheduling sex. Knowing that set days were their sex days would take the pressure off, he argued. On Tuesday, Thursday, and Sunday they would maintain their schedule with an option to increase the days as wished.

This sounded like as much fun as making a contract to take the garbage out.

A slight touch startled her. Amro's fingertip resonated a tingle on her left hand. "Can I get you another cappuccino?"

"No. I don't normally drink those so fast. I wouldn't be able to sleep if I had another one."

"I thought you said that we weren't going to sleep tonight."

"I did say that, didn't I?" She slid her arm closer to her cappuccino, trying to get the upper hand again.

"Amro how do you know the guard?"

"There's nothing mysterious going on here, Olivia. Don't let your mind make connections just because I'm Egyptian."

"Then tell me how you know the guard."

"If it will set your mind at ease, I'll tell you. It's really not complicated. He's a friend of my uncle."

"And why were you at the fundraiser? I understood it was only a short list of significant people."

He gave her a scolding look. "I'll try to ignore that you don't consider me a significant person. My father has a background with Egyptian art. The guard made arrangements for me to meet with Rebecca. She invited me to the fundraiser."

Olivia wondered if Rebecca was bright enough to realize that two unknown people had been invited to the fundraiser because their also unknown fathers had a connection with the art world. Fortunately, she hadn't left any contact information.

"Did you leave any contact information with Rebecca?"

Amro raised his eyebrows with the appreciation of engaging with a worthy chess player. "Of course not."

"That's very intelligent."

Two lanky guys from one of the inhabited tables, scooted back their chairs, piled books into their backpacks, and meandered out along the sidewalk. They did a double take at the limo parked outside and looked around for a glimpse at the significant people that would be attached to it. Their scope did not take in Olivia and Amro at the coffee shop.

Putting her pride aside, Olivia thought that the ability to blend in could come in handy in the future.

"Olivia… I'm curious what you know about Egyptian art."

"Well, my father was a collector," she claimed. Always good to keep the story consistent since she didn't know how tight he'd gotten with Rebecca.

"Of Egyptian art?"

"No, he had a strong interest in Egyptian art, but he was more of a European collector."

"And what do you know about Egyptian art?"

She gave him a coy smile. "Not as much as I'd like to. Are you familiar with this artifact that was suppose to be unveiled tonight?"

"Absolutely."

"Do you think it was really connected to King Tut's mother?"

He looked down at his water and shook his head in agreement.

"Wow! This is amazing!" Olivia was no longer being coy. She wanted to know more about the faience. "I'm not as familiar with this time period of art. What do you know about this?"

"The faience, or tjehnet, is considered magical. It's associated with light and creation by some. Others believe it to be associated with temple and funerals. The faience we didn't see tonight is a turquoise bowl with a lotus figure."

"Have you seen it before?"

"Yes."

"How did you see it? It was never exhibited!"

He studied her quick reaction and smiled. "It was on the website for awhile."

"Oh, of course."

His eyes acknowledged that she didn't trust him.

She didn't care. Why should she trust him? They had only known each other for a few hours, under some very strange circumstances.

"Why is the faience considered magical? I've heard about this thing with Egyptian artifacts and mummies being magical. But I'm not sure if any of this is true."

"Believe it Olivia. If you studied Egyptian culture, you would find that it's one of the most ancient and highly developed cultures in history. It's not just about an artifact or a beautiful bowl. When the Kings reigned, Egypt was a ruler. We ruled through the most sophisticated architecture, agriculture, and military. And there was one of most important factors during this rule …"

She was hooked on his recount of his country's golden era.

Again he looked down at his water as if contemplating whether to continue.

"What was that factor?"

"Magic." His eyes connected with hers and she unable to look away from the golden brown topaz that made her think about the eternal gold surrounding mummies.

"Magic?"

"Egyptians were the religious owners of magic. It was practiced at a high level. Worlds blending between reality and supernatural."

She felt goose bumps on her arm as he continued.

"The energy from this magical and enlightened period, a time of amazing power and prestige, is forever stored in the artifacts, mummies, and tombs of that reign. Those who respect this will be blessed."

"And the ones who don't respect it?"

"They will experience the Egyptian curse." His brow deepened into a punishing frown.

"What happens to those who are cursed?"

"The same thing that happened to the Museum director."

For the first time she felt a little nervous. She checked to make sure the limo was still waiting.

He touched her arm gently. "Don't be nervous. The curse is not my idea. It's been documented throughout history. Mummy raiders have suffered the consequences of their disrespect. If you don't believe me, Google it later tonight."

"I will. But why do you think the Museum director was cursed?""

He was a part of stealing the faience from Egypt. Rather than being a tomb raider, he just went through some other channels. But his hands are as dirty as those who took the faience from Egyptian soil."

"You don't think he was murdered?"

"The curse comes about in many ways. He may or may not have been murdered, but I promise you the curse is behind it."

"We're really presuming too much. Maybe he had a heart attack or blood clot and died of natural causes."

"There's nothing natural about it."

She stirred the remaining foam of her empty cappuccino. What are the chances that the director would die at the exact moment of an historical unveiling at a private event surrounded by media speculation and unfavorable comments from the head of Egyptian antiquities?

Her heart jumped as she recalled when she and Jonathon were first talking about the faience. After her blushing with excitement at the thought of seeing the artifact, Jonathon had suggested that she was under the Egyptian spell.

"Amro, is there a difference between the spell and the curse?"

"Yes, of course."

"How is the spell different?"

"The spell is from the magic. It's like an energy that draws you in."

"Is that bad, like the curse?"

He laughed at her innocence. "Every Egyptian is under the spell. And those who experience the Egyptian artifacts or mummies easily fall under the spell. What matters is which side you're on. Those who act with respect or those who do not."

She wondered if her ex-fiancé Miles had acted with respect and remembered their conversation at the restaurant. He had talked about museums having the right to purchase artifacts that "crossed a few bridges."

Had his hands gotten dirty also with the faience?

EIGHT

Her concern for Miles' welfare distracted her as Amro continued to talk about Egyptian tomb raiders and their ultimate demise. Apparently there was no place to hide if the curse was put upon you from your own greedy actions. Tomb raiders were found dead near their spoiled site, along the sandy trail to their escape route, or in another country. There were even stories about an infamous anthropologist whose pet mysteriously died immediately after him.

Knowing her ex-fiancé, she doubted that Miles believed any of these stories. He would categorize them as propaganda to dissuade raiders and art dealers.

"Amro are some of these tomb raiders Egyptian?"

"Yes, some are. But more are from other cultures. They have less belief in the power of the curse."

"But if the curse is so strong and so widely believed in Egyptian culture, why would an Egyptian be a raider?"

"Greed. Or desperation. These are the only things that make a man do such a foolish thing. To risk his life. And his after life."

"His after life?"

"Yes, our longer life after we leave this world."

"So the curse is believed to follow the raider after death?"

He nodded and sat back in his chair, crossing his legs.

"How do Egyptians see the after life?"

Sighing lightly, he picked at an invisible piece of fuzz on his pant leg. "You're a very easy girl to talk to Olivia. But I don't want to bore you with a long talk about religion."

Maybe he felt he'd already shared too much. She could tell from his crossed legs and folded arms that she wasn't going to get any more information from him tonight.

She needed to make sure that he would want to see her another night.

"Well I am getting a little tired and need to get home."

"You have a little doggy to let out before bedtime?" he teased.

"No, but I do plan on getting a dog soon."

"You should. He'd be a lucky little dog."

She smiled. "Can we drop you off somewhere?"

"Sure."

As they entered the limo, he gave the driver directions. After fifteen minutes of casual conversation, they pulled up to a gas station.

"You live at a gas station?"

"No, but my roommate would freak out if he saw me dropped off in a limo. I really don't think it would be a good idea."

"So the roommate is a he?"

He grinned. "Yes, it's a he. Jealous already?"

"Just asking."

"Thanks for the ride, Olivia."

He leaned in and gave her a light hug that sent electricity through her. "I need your number." Pulling his cell phone from his pocket, his patient topaz eyes waited confidently.

She gave it to him.

He returned the favor by immediately calling her number so she would have his also.

NINE

Sunday morning was one of her favorite mornings ... no early morning jog, no rushing to work, no guilt-inducing call from her Mom to attend Shabbat service at temple. Her Mom had converted to Judaism when she married her second husband Al who adopted Olivia after her father disappeared to Greece.

The shift from Olivia Pappas to Olivia Katz was easy. Her Stepfather was doting, supportive, and brought laughter to their home for a while. When he died of a heart attack when she was twenty, Olivia never considered changing her name back. She and her Mom carried on the Katz name.

Slowly drifting awake she thought about the evening before at the Museum and Amro.

When her phone rang, she dug through her purse for it breaking a nail. "Hello?"

"Liv, are you alright?" It was Jonathon.

"Yes of course. Why?"

"Why are you so grumpy in the morning?"

She didn't want to tell him that she was disappointed that the call wasn't from Amro. Then she'd have to explain this new guy and how they met.

"Did you read this morning's *St. Louis Sun Journal?*"

"I'll call you back in fifteen minutes." She pulled on some clothes and her ball cap and headed to the newsstand. Omar was there as always and smiled with his dependable good nature.

Back in the apartment, she unfolded the paper and searched the inside sections. When he rang back she still hadn't found the story.

"What section is it in?"

"The front page."

"What?" She flipped the pages back as the advertisements and the sports section hit the floor with a thud.

A bold font stretched across the top of the page: *Museum Director Dies at Private Party.*

She read on.

St. Louis, Missouri – The museum director for the local Art Museum was discovered dead beside the exhibit of a disputed Egyptian artifact.

Nearly 100 guests were in attendance at a private party for an elite group of donors and community leaders. The event's highlight was reported to be the unveiling of a newly acquired Egyptian bowl that the head of Egyptian antiquities, Dr. Hasaneen, has claimed to be stolen from the excavation site.

Dr. Hasaneen asserted that the 3000-year-old bowl vanished from a storage facility near Cairo. The bowl was next seen on the St. Louis museum's website as the featured artifact of the heavily promoted new Egyptian Exhibit.

The museum director, Art Schneider, 47, died of unknown causes beside the empty exhibit.

A spokesperson for the museum stated that the artifact is in safekeeping.

The coroner's report is pending.

"Liv, you there…?"

"Front page…" she muttered to herself.

"I know. Finally. It seems you have to die to get on the front page of the *St. Louis Sun Journal.*"

"Have you heard from the Museum?"

"Not yet. We'll probably get called together tomorrow for some sort of rally the troops or don't talk to the media meeting."

"Is the faience really safe?"

"Yes. I broke down and called Miles. He says it's locked up safe and sound."

"Good."

"Liv, did you go to the fundraiser last night?"

"Yes."

"Oops."

"What? Why oops?"

"Honey, if this is a murder, everyone at that event will be questioned."

The paper slipped from her hand. The Arts & Entertainment section dropped onto the fallen Sports pages. A hushed splat echoed throughout her silent apartment draped in shadows of the rising sun.

"Did you give them your contact information?"

"No. And I used an alias."

"That could be good if they can't find you. If they do, an alias is going to be really hard to explain."

"I didn't know anyone there."

"Did you keep a low profile?"

She remembered Rebecca prancing her around as the New York tycoon's daughter, endless interest about her father's art, and being scurried out the back door.

"Not exactly. But I was only introduced by my alias."

"Were they taking photos at the event?"

"One of the Museum's PR staffers was collecting little groups to take photos. But I wasn't in any of those."

"You know sometimes they like to take candid shots of the event participants."

Was it her imagination or did the shadows in the apartment deepen?

TEN

Returning to work on Monday felt reassuring. A dose of the normal. As normal as it gets at an agency. Account managers were yelling at two account executives because they had gotten yelled at by the client. A VP had slammed his door closed and had his head resting in his crossed arms on the desk, lamenting the loss of a major account that would result in layoffs. And the receptionist had just called in to quit without notice.

It was still much better than the thought of getting questioned by police investigating a probable murder of the leader of one of the top cultural centers in St. Louis.

She settled in to her workstation ready to lose herself in the unrelenting projects. Her Blackberry vibrated.

Couldn't her creative director look outside of his office to see that she was here already? But the text was from Amro - *Cairo News just did a story about the Museum Director. Call me.*

She dropped the phone in her pocket and scurried to the bathroom.

"Hi Amro, it's Olivia."

"Why are you whispering?"

"I'm in the bathroom at work."

"This thing is going to get crazy Olivia."

"I have the same feeling."

The bathroom door opened as her co-worker Sharon entered, scoped out her phone, and slipped into one of the stalls.

"Mom, I'll bring the roaster over after work. I know you need it sooner, but I can't get away today."

"Someone in the bathroom?"

"Yes Mom you're right."

"Ok, let's get together after work. We need to develop a plan."

"Sure. I'll call you when I'm on my way."

Olivia looked in the mirror and pretended to fix her hair as her co-worker washed her hands. "Gotta love mothers."

Sharon gave her a half smile. "It's gonna be a bitch today. Did you hear we just lost the big account?"

"I heard."

But her mind wasn't on the account. There was much more at stake for her right now.

<hr />

After work, she rushed to her car and called Amro. They decided to meet at the same Starbucks. When she arrived, he was sitting at the table they had sat at on Saturday after the fundraiser.

She joined him.

"Do you want a coffee Olivia?"

"Not yet, I'm too anxious to see this Egyptian news you talked about."

He handed her his Blackberry which showed the Egyptian news website story:

Museum Director of Stolen Faience Dies

Cairo, Egypt – The museum director of the stolen Egyptian faience has died without explanation at a museum party for large donors. The museum in St. Louis, Missouri, in the United States, refused to return the faience that was stolen from a storage facility near Cairo.

Reports from St. Louis divulged that the faience would have been unveiled if not for the sudden death of the director found next to the faience's empty exhibit. The museum stated that the faience is in safekeeping.

Dr. Hasaneen demands that the faience be returned immediately.

"The faience must be returned to Egyptian soil. We cannot tolerate this flagrant raiding of our national treasures. As many raiders have seen before, the power of the curse will only cause destruction until the magnificent faience is returned. The faience must be returned immediately."

Olivia returned the Blackberry to Amro. "Do you think the destruction will continue?"

"It will."

She bit her lower lip, a childhood habit that she had broken years ago. Her concern for Miles was growing.

Amro folded her hand in his, softly stroking the crest below her thumb. "We're linked Olivia. And we have to be very careful or we could face trouble unlike any we've ever imagined."

"What kind of trouble?"

"Accusations. Questions. Prison."

"Prison?"

"They'll need someone to blame this death on. I don't think the police are strong believers in the curse."

For the first time she was truly nervous. "What can we do?"

"First, we tell no one that we know each other. Your chauffeur on Saturday – do you know him or was that a rental?"

"Rental."

"Good."

He continued stroking her hand. "Next, we stay away from the museum. No visits. No phone calls."

"For how long?"

"Indefinitely."

She wondered how she would ever see the faience. If only she could see it just one time.

"Promise me, Olivia."

She looked up and locked eyes with him. Perhaps she could get out of police accusations. For him, it would be much harder. But hiding would make her look less innocent. Not talking to anyone about this man who had fallen into her life would make her more vulnerable.

"Olivia, do you promise?"

She wondered what would have happened had his friend, the guard, not helped them escape out the back door. Did the police gather the names of the people remaining? Had she not been whisked away she would have had to make a choice to lie to them or confess her real name.

"I owe you that much Amro. You did help me avoid an unpleasant introduction to the police the other night."

He kissed her hand. "How can you look so beautiful after working all day?"

She laughed. "Stress agrees with me."

"And you agree with me," he pressed her hand against his cheek.

She soaked up his touch. The Egyptian magic was in more than just historical artifacts.

ELEVEN

Her Blackberry interrupted their connection. She slipped her hand from Amro's and checked her phone. It was Jonathon.

"I better get this." She walked to the window for better reception.

"What's up Jonathon?"

"Olivia, I don't know where you are or what you're doing but you have to come over to my place right away."

"I'm a little busy right now."

"Ok, be at my place in thirty minutes. I'll explain everything then."

The non-negotiable click ended the conversation.

Something must have happened at the Museum. As much as she wanted to continue to be with Amro, she needed to find out what was going on with Jonathon.

She slid back into her seat. "I have to head out soon. Urgent matter."

He nodded.

"Can I walk you to your car?"

The heat soaked into her shirt within a block. Beside her car, Amro circled his arm around her waist. She ever so gently pulled away. Cultural and religious differences aside, her intuition told her to be cautious with this entirely too handsome man.

"Sure you need to take care of the urgent matter?"

She nodded affirmatively.

"Ok Olivia. Call me."

As she turned the corner to the street leading to Jonathon's condo, she muttered to herself, "This better be good Jonathon."

Street parking was already taken, so she drove the three blocks to her apartment and walked to his place. He buzzed her in the building. As usual his door was slightly ajar to welcome her.

She knocked lightly and let herself in. He gave her a little hug. "Someone is perspiring a bit," he noted.

"No street parking over here." She didn't mention the other reason she was still hot.

"Let me get you a cold lemonade."

He handed her a glass of his fresh squeezed specialty.

"Jonathon, what's going on?"

"Have a seat. This could take a minute. What time is it?" He glanced over at his art deco antique clock. "Nine-thirty. Good. We need to watch the news at 10."

She raised her eyebrow. Jonathon was not much of a news fanatic.

"Miles' interview will likely be on it."

"Miles' interview?"

"Yes, the Museum was swarming with media today and Miles was assigned to talk to the media. Normally, the director would do that, but he's busy getting his autopsy."

"Ouch."

"That was pretty cold. Sorry. I'm just on edge. Everyone was on edge today." He took a couple gulps of his lemonade. "Olivia, I've never seen anything like it. Media was crawling around the Museum front entrance like circling vultures. They were following employees to their cars as we tried to escape out the back entrance, absolutely bombarding the poor staff with questions that we had sworn on our lives not to answer. Finally, the guards had to escort us. Then, when sacrificial Miles was doing an interview on the front steps, they all ran to the front, and a mass exit of employees made it to their cars unadulterated."

She touched his hand reassuringly. "How awful."

Crunching an ice cube, he muttered, "Now I know how those poor celebrities feel when the paparazzi won't leave them alone. I don't think I'm equipped to be a star."

He looked up at the clock. "Nearly ten, let's turn on the TV."

The perfectly groomed forty-something male news anchor teased, "The Art Museum director dies at a private museum event. Questions are flying. Stay tuned for the story of a century at ten."

Jonathon flipped to the other news stations in time to catch the tail end of similar teases.

"Every station covered this?" Olivia was getting unnerved.

"And radio stations and newspapers."

"Jeez."

Miles' image came on screen.

Jonathon reached for the remote and turned up the volume.

A young female reporter was talking a little too fast to the anchor. "Yes, Jim, we had a chance to talk with the chief curator earlier today. Here's what he had to say…" They switched to the taped story.

"Mr. Sanders, can you tell us when the Egyptian treasure will be recovered?"

"Recovered? The faience is not in the process of being recovered. It's safe and sound under museum security."

"But Mr. Sanders, if the Egyptian treasure is safe, why has no one seen it since the Museum took possession of it. Other than a brief photo on the website that was taken down."

Jonathon and Olivia stared helplessly at the television.

"Miss, I assure you that the faience is safe."

"Then why would the Museum director be murdered right before it was expected to be unveiled?

"We do not have confirmation that he was murdered."

"So you believe he was murdered?"

"The coroner's report is pending."

"When will the report be released?"

"Sometime this week I believe."

"And when will the public have the chance to see for themselves that the Museum has possession of the Egyptian treasure?"

"Miss, I need to take care of some business. We appreciate your concern and will be back with you on that." Miles slipped into the Museum and away from the unrelenting questions.

"So Jim, there you have it. We have no assurance that the Egyptian treasure wasn't stolen. And we're waiting for the coroner's report on the director's cause of death."

"Excellent reporting Jennifer. I'm sure you'll be following up on this one."

"Absolutely Jim."

The two anchors gave one another a dramatic look of concern before moving on to the next story.

Jonathon buried his head in his hands. "This is awful."

Olivia comforted him, rubbing his shoulder. But she was far from comfortable. "This might not be a good time to talk about this."

"What?"

"I'm worried about Miles."

"Me too. This stress level is crazy. And who knows what impact this could have on his career if the Board doesn't think he handles it right."

"No, I'm worried about his … well, his safety."

"Safety?" Jonathon sat up.

"Do you believe in the Egyptian curse?"

"I'm familiar with the history of it. And I'd have to say it appears to be validated. Tomb raiders and those connected to them haven't done well soon after their act."

"Do you think it's possible that the director was a victim of the Egyptian curse?"

Jonathon's glass of lemonade slipped, splashing the sticky liquid onto his couch. The consummate clean freak, he grabbed a napkin and dabbed it up before facing her again. "It's possible Liv."

"And if that's the case, do you think Miles might have helped in any way that would make him connected to the act?"

His lemonade tipped out of his neglectful grip again. He ignored the sticky stain penetrating his immaculate couch. "My god, could this get any worse?"

"I hope not. Let's just hope not."

But the feeling did not go away, and Olivia knew she would have another night of restlessness.

⁓

The next day, talk in the agency break room had switched gears from the gloom and doom of lost accounts to a betting war on who killed the art museum director.

"Come on Olivia, who do you think murdered the director?" Sharon prodded.

"We don't know that he was murdered."

"Please, he dies suddenly before the Egyptian treasure is unveiled. Haven't you read any good murder mysteries Olivia?"

"Plenty."

"Well, I think it was the Egyptian dude that wanted it back. He certainly seemed pissed enough to off the director." Sharon smiled smugly.

A new account executive wadded up his devoured bag of Doritos. "Are you crazy Sharon? He's too high profile to get his hands dirty. Maybe it was that Museum curator they interviewed yesterday. Now that the director is bumped, he might go after his job and get credit for the Museum's hot new treasure."

Olivia stared in disbelief.

A bubbly intern jumped up and threw her arms in the air cheerleader style. "It was some religious martyr that's behind the scenes. Someone who would want to punish the director for stealing Egyptian property."

"Wait a minute." Sharon tapped the table with her yogurt-laced spoon. "I have a second idea. The dude who sold the bowl to the Museum. You know, the art dealer. Maybe he's trying to cover his tracks. He must have made a killing on this deal. Oops, a killing," she giggled. "Get it."

No one laughed.

"Fine. It was kinda funny. I've gotta get back to work." Sharon huffed out of the room.

Another intern, a consummate suck-up, crooned at her, "I want to know what Olivia thinks."

"I think it's time to get back to work." She escaped the room that had a sickening odor of Doritos and the intern's grape gum. Although she didn't share much about her personal life with her agency colleagues, she was surprised that no one remembered that the Museum curator was her ex-fiancé.

But she was more worried about the growing talk and sentiment of St. Louisans especially those who had influence over Miles and the return the faience.

Could the list of suspects be the same for viewers of last night's news? She expected Dr. Hasaneen to be on the list considering his heated request to return the faience. And another unnamed martyr was a predictable shortlist. But Miles? How could anyone think that someone would kill his or her boss for a promotion? If the bantering of break rooms throughout St. Louis were tracking this way, Miles could become a victim of a witch-hunt.

How would he get himself out of this escalating debacle?

She decided to call him after work.

As she opened her desktop folders and started to work on yet another annual report, she paused her mouse mid-click... the art dealer.

Could Sharon have had an inspired moment of insight? Maybe all those murder mysteries she read had her on to something. The art dealer had motivation. He would want to save his reputation to continue his lucrative career. The director knew all the details.

The director and Miles.

But the director was in the hot seat and more apt to bow under the pressure, pointing the finger to another to redirect the scrutiny. The art dealer, naturally, was in the hot seat next.

The Museum had yet to disclose the name of the dealer, only referring to him as a reputable French-Lebanese art dealer.

She ran her hand through her dark hair, clearing her mind. Work had to get done. Still, her thoughts drifted back to the faience throughout the day. By the end of day, she realized the client's annual report had started to take on a middle-eastern look. That just didn't make sense for a Midwest dairy association.

Tomorrow would be an early morning so she could get some redesign completed before the noon deadline. Tonight she wanted to check in with Miles.

And maybe give Amro a call. She smiled at the thought.

After grabbing a quick to-go sandwich, pretzels, and yogurt at the corner deli, she drudged up the three flights to her unadorned apartment. She was too embarrassed to have friends over to her under-decorated surroundings. There was an expectation that a graphic designer have a hip and artsy space more like Jonathon or Miles' condos. But she had no interest in designing this "temporary" apartment that she'd been living in for five years. So she met friends at their place or out somewhere. There was enough pressure at work to provide fabulous design.

Finishing the last bite of tuna salad sandwich, she called Miles. It rang. And rang some more. No answer.

Not one to leave messages, Olivia clicked the phone off.

Poor Miles. He was probably hiding under the bed.

The vibration of her phone caught her attention. Thinking it was Miles, she answered, "Hey sweetie, how are you?"

"It's Jonathon. Were you trying to call Miles?" My god, he was good. She sighed lightly, "Yes, oh psychic one."

"Psychic? Not so much. Just observant."

"Do I usually call Miles sweetie?"

"When you're being a sweetie."

She laughed.

"Sorry to break the mood here, but I just saw another tease for the late news."

"Miles was interviewed again?"

"Not this time. They snatched an interview with a guest that attended the infamous fundraiser the night our director died."

"I'm on my way over."

TWELVE

The perfectly groomed forty-something male news anchor had just finished a tease when Olivia rushed into Jonathon's apartment. The young female reporter who had interviewed Miles was rapidly talking to the live camera, "We're outside the Art Museum where our attempts to interview the curator this evening were unsuccessful…"

"It's ten o'clock at night. The Museum is closed," Jonathon shouted at his platinum hi-def television.

Olivia patted his leg to quiet him.

"However, earlier today we interviewed a museum benefactor who was a guest at the fundraiser the night the Museum director was murdered."

The anchor cleared his throat and corrected her, "The night the Museum director was 'allegedly' murdered. I believe we're still waiting for the coroner's report?"

"Oh, yes Jim, that's right. My apologies. And now to the interview from earlier today at the home of Marilyn Wentworth."

The camera had a wide view allowing viewers to see the elaborate backdrop of Mrs. Wentworth's mansion in Clayton – a suburb that reminded Olivia of a miniature San Francisco with more sedate rolling hills, high end commerce, agencies including her employer, and some of the most valuable property that old money could buy.

Mrs. Wentworth was conservatively dressed in an expensive suit - ankles neatly tucked together in a text-book Miss Manners' style - complimented by dark Italian shoes that contrasted with the white marble floors. The living room soared two stories high. Curved windows showed a hint of a garden with a fountain comparable to municipal botanical gardens.

Money was nearly falling into the camera lens.

The young reporter, positioned on the couch next to her in a Barbara Walters style, modeled the same concerned look. Was she going to get her to cry, Olivia wondered?

"Mrs. Wentworth, I understand you were at the Museum the night the director died?"

"Yes dear, my husband and I have been long time supporters of the exceptional work of the art Museum. We were deeply saddened by the director's death. He was a gifted administrator who was dedicated to enhancing the Museum's deserved recognition in the art world."

Jonathon slapped his leg and laughed, "Good luck with this one, missy reporter." His newly established animosity for the media was growing by the day. She knew he was being protective, but really she felt they were just doing their job. Best to keep that to herself at the moment though.

"Mrs. Wentworth, do you believe the Egyptian treasure was improperly purchased?"

She patted the young reporter's arm, "My goodness no, dear. The Museum is absolutely ethical. My husband and I would never contribute to a cause that wasn't."

"Somebody's covering their ass," Jonathon interjected.

The reporter continued, "But ma'am, for the first time in the St. Louis museum's history the purchase of an artifact has been considered questionably purchased and a stolen piece?"

Mrs. Wentworth blinked for a moment before returning the volley. "Dear, whom did you hear that from?"

Caught off guard, the reporter responded, "We don't divulge sources ma'am."

"Well, please check that. It is the belief of my husband and I that this purchase was absolutely pure. Now, I must get to my next meeting, dear. However, we do want to express our condolences to the staff of the Art Museum who are enduring so much at this difficult time. We know the St. Louis community is supporting them and our wonderful Museum that has been a cultural cornerstone. "

The reporter, having been checkmated, wrapped up the interview with a promise for more information in the coming days.

"Geez, Mrs. Wentworth could have a job in public relations anytime," Olivia marveled.

"She doesn't need a job. Her husband is one of the wealthiest men in St. Louis, perhaps the country. He was invited by the president to be an ambassador, and turned it down."

She let out a long whistle.

"Got that right. Now let me get you a lemonade."

"Score one for the Museum."

"Finally."

He came back to the couch handing her a lemonade and wrapping his legs comfortably over hers. "Even if the Museum is guilty of purchasing the faience from a disreputable dealer, I don't want to see a solid reputation forever damaged."

"Jonathon, are you starting to take Miles' side?"

"No. Really no. I just would like to find a way to get this all cleared up so everyone could be happy and this turmoil would be over."

"But you don't think it was right for the Museum to have purchased the faience if they knew the trail was questionable?"

"I'm completely opposed to bending those rules. Just wishing there was some way to reverse this crazy situation."

"Well they could always just return it to Egypt."

"After all this? The Board will be completely adamant about not returning it."

"Why?"

"Admission of guilt. Culpability. Their reputation. Need I go on?"

"I get the point."

They sipped lemonade sitting comfortably in silence as only old friends can do. Olivia finished hers first and took the glass to the sink. She checked the time and grabbed her purse.

"Early morning at the agency tomorrow."

He kissed her cheek as she leaned down for a goodnight hug.

At the door, she turned back to see Jonathon deep in thought.

"Jonathon, do you think the faience is really secure at the Museum given all this publicity?"

He nodded affirmatively.

"Where do they keep something that valuable?"

"Top Secret."

"What if someone wanted to steal it?"

"Liv! Thanks a lot. Now I won't get any sleep tonight."

She slipped out the door, blowing him an apologetic kiss.

THIRTEEN

‹⁓›

Two hours after getting into work, Olivia had revised her oddly middle-eastern design of the dairy association annual report to a more appropriate apple pie and baseball look. As she e-mailed her draft to her creative director, her Blackberry vibrated with an incoming text message. Her heart jumped when she saw it was Amro. *Cairo News confirmed that the faience is King Tut's mysterious mother! Dr. Hasaneen declared this to be an artifact of national significance and the find of centuries. Check out the news video link. Call me.*

Olivia looked around at the surrounding workstations. Her co-workers were in design mode listening to their iPods. She rummaged through her purse as if she couldn't find something, and then grabbed her car keys, mouthing to one of the designers that she'd be right back. He nodded without interest.

Her car was baking in the mid-morning sun. She had the second best parking deal at the agency – off street, paid for parking. The best was the underground parking reserved for the executives. Today second best worked to her advantage since she could get satellite reception above ground.

The car door squeaked slightly showing a hint of its age. She tossed her keys on the console, grabbed her Blackberry from her pocket, and clicked on the news video link.

Dr. Hasaneen was fired up for another interview. As she listened to him declare without pause that the faience belonged to the mysterious mother of King Tut, she was stunned by the logo on the microphone in the shot – BBC.

Frozen in the seat of her sweltering hot car, she jumped when her phone rang.

"Amro?" she managed to whisper.

"Olivia. You OK?"

"I don't feel well."

"That's two of us. Olivia this is just starting I'm pretty sure."

"It's going to get worse?" Her voice struck an unusual high note.

"How could it not? There hasn't been anything bigger than this in the art world in many people's lifetime."

"True. But I just don't know what's going to happen next."

"You have to remain strong Olivia. And it's very important that you remember what we talked about."

"Talked about?"

"At Starbucks, remember?"

She was coming out of her haze of shock. "Yes. Yes."

"And that was?"

"We don't tell anyone we know each other."

"And?"

"And we stay away from the Art Museum."

"Right!" She could hear the smile on his face. "You're amazing Olivia!"

She saw the time on the clock tower across the street. "I gotta get back to work. They'll be looking for me."

"Get going then. Olivia?"

"Yes?"

"Be strong."

"I will Amro."

She heard him send her a kiss before they clicked off their phones.

As she slipped back to her workstation, one the designers looked up and saw she had come back empty-handed. She raised her eyebrows, questioning. Olivia shrugged her shoulders as if she hadn't found it. In the world of design, unrefined sign language was preferred to disconnecting from iPods.

Olivia opened up her next project folder. Finally something other than annual reports – a tradeshow exhibit screen for a beer company. Although she complained to Jonathon and Miles that her job was blocking her from her dream of becoming a real artist, she had to admit that she loved the variety of projects and creating for different clients. Structure for an artist doesn't come naturally. Would she be able to create on her own, without looming deadlines and a creative director breathing down her neck?

Her collection of ceramics from her college days was tucked in the back of her closet. It had been years since she had created any art outside of the agency. Even talking about becoming an artist seemed fraudulent.

Still, she hadn't given up on her dream of becoming an artist.

Lately she found herself dreaming more about the faience. Since the night at Jonathon's when she had seen the breathtaking photos, she awakened with the glimpse of the brilliant blue lotus floating in her memory.

What would it be like to create a piece of art of such beauty, such magic? She wondered if the artist had any idea how significant his work was? Since it appeared that the piece was made for King Tut's mother, it would have been an established artist.

She switched her iPod music to her newly down-loaded Egyptian music. To her surprise her music search had found a contemporary artist with a similar name to Amro. Amr Diab, an Egyptian rock star, was as beautiful as he was talented. As she listened to his music, she imagined being in Egypt when the faience was being created for the young King's mother.

She envisioned the artist, working alone in a small hut sheltered from the unrelenting sun, sand swirling about his sandaled feet as he bent over his ceramic masterpiece intent to create not only a work of the highest quality but art that would make the beautiful young woman gasp from its beauty and magic…

"Olivia. Hey, snap out of it," Sharon interrupted.

"What?"

"Where were you? I was standing here calling your name three times!"

"Sorry. What's up?"

"The royal highness, our wonderful creative director, wants to see you," she slurred with sarcasm.

Olivia grabbed a notebook and pen, preparing to take notes on the next emergency project, and headed to his office.

But her mind was still on the faience. How was she going to keep her promise to Amro and stay away from the Museum? That would mean she would never actually see the faience in person.

Could she really say no to an opportunity to see the object of her dreams?

FOURTEEN

Olivia had just started her new assignment from her creative director when the e-mail pop-up caught her attention. She rarely got e-mail from Jonathon at her work address. The agency didn't really have a problem with personal e-mail, but with the intense workload she so rarely responded that friends usually would text her or call. Knowing her so well, Jonathon had sent it in urgent mode. The little red exclamation point caught her eye.

Stopped to pick up paper for you at newsstand but the paper had sold out. When did that happen last? Here's the link to the online version of the St. Louis Sun Journal instead.

Poor Miles. Passed by him in the hall today. He was rushing somewhere. He looked like hell Olivia! I've never seen Miles like this. I think he needs us. Not sure what to do, but we'll figure it out. – Jonathon

Honestly she hadn't read this much news at one time since… She couldn't remember when. The link to the media story opened.

Rumors of Egyptian Curse at Museum Spreads

BBC reports that Egyptian head of antiquities, Dr. Hasaneen, claims that the St. Louis Museum's role in the suspicious acquisition of a rare Egyptian artifact brings the shadow of the curse on key players surrounding the faience. Dr. Hasaneen also shocked the international art world with the declaration that the artifact belonged to the mysterious mother of King Tut.

Artifacts during this reign and in particular associated with King Tut are valued at the highest levels. King Tut's mother's tomb has yet to be discovered. Objects from her tomb would be valued beyond speculation. The belief that this singular artifact is connected with her would make it of even greater value.

Dr. Hasaneen referred to the late director of the St. Louis museum as a tomb raider. Historically, Egyptian tomb raiders have met their demise through natural or unusual causes believed to have stemmed from the curse.

Olivia felt goose bumps forming along her arms. "Miles…" she accidentally whispered aloud.

One of the designers, annoyed by the disruption, pulled an iPod earplug from his right ear, "What?"

"Oh, nothing. Sorry Josh."

He nodded, replugged, and returned to his design.

But she couldn't get back into her work, deadline or no deadline. She was absolutely sure that Miles was in danger now.

And he would be the last person to accept this or to try to reverse it.

Jonathon was right. Miles needed them.

FIFTEEN

The next morning Olivia arrived at the office energized from a full night's sleep. Exhaustion from thinking about tomb raiders, death, and media had finally become her friend and slipped her into a deep sleep.

Today she just wanted to revel in a day of regimen – catch up on the new project, tidy up her work area, listen to her favorite songs on her iPod, and appreciate the predictable chaos of the agency.

Clearing all the items from her workstation desk onto her chair and the floor, she looked around for the department cleaning supplies. Missing in action as usual. Supplies had a way of disappearing at the agency. But the chaos and project triage made finding a petty theft a low priority.

She headed to the bathroom to grab some paper towels. A few moist paper towels finished off with some dry ones would do the trick. A least it would get rid of the worst of the dust and coffee rings.

Armed with one hand of moist towels and another hand of dry, she looped her finger around the bathroom door just as it swung open, nearly scraping her sandaled feet.

"Oh, shit, sorry Olivia, " Sharon didn't slow down as she slipped behind the toilet door. "I was about to pee my pants after stopping to watch that crazy news in the break room. Or as we're suppose to say, the staff lounge. When they start serving martinis, then I'll call it the staff lounge. Meanwhile, let's call it what it is – a break room..."

Dared she ask what the news was?

"Sharon?"

The flush blocked her from asking more before Sharon opened the stall door, threw a little soap and water on her hands and briskly dried them with paper towels.

"Cat got your tongue?"

"No. I was just wondering what was so interesting on the news."

"A media frenzy at the Art Museum. Never saw anything like it in St. Louis. The Pope didn't even get this much attention. There's so much media on the front steps of the Museum, they're going to trip over each other and roll down Art Hill into the pond. Then they'll be rolling down the hill to cover that..." Sharon left the bathroom cackling at her own joke.

Olivia rushed to the staff lounge. The television was full blast and surrounded by a standing-room-only crowd. She squeezed past a tall intern to get a view of the screen just as a live interview with Miles came on. The CNN reporter was pounding him with questions. Then BBC, CBS, ABC, and *The New York Times* joined in the free-for-all...

"Do you think the Museum director was murdered?

When will the autopsy report be disclosed?

Do you think the Egyptian curse caused the director's death?

Are you sure the faience is safe?

When will the public have a chance to see this artifact?

Do you think anyone else is at risk of the Egyptian curse?

How does the benefactor feel about this suspicious procurement?

Will this harm the Museum's reputation?

Is this really a method to draw attention to your Museum?

Are you and Dr. Hasaneen collaborating on this?

How does the director's family feel about his label as a tomb raider?

Can you respond to Dr. Hasaneen's declaration that this is an artifact from King Tut's mother's tomb?

Are there any plans to return the faience to Egypt?

As curator, do you consider yourself a tomb raider also?"

Miles was staring mutely at the media as if a descending tornado was in his path. From the shadowed entrance of the Museum, a staffer, probably from the Public Relations department, came to his rescue.

Holding her hand up like a police officer directing traffic, she pushed her way through the microphones, cameras, and reporters and shouted in a firm voice. "Ladies and gentlemen, this has gotten completely out of hand. This press conference is now postponed. Please contact my office for a statement or a personal interview."

She ushered Miles into the safety of the Museum as the media shouted it's outrage and continued with a litany of questions directed at his back.

The CNN reporter faced the camera. "So there you have it. The Museum refused to answer any questions on this escalating story of international concern. And we might say at this point, of international outrage. We will get back to you with further developments."

The Breaking News banner dropped from the screen as regular programming returned.

One of the designers, Josh, turned and asked, "Hey Olivia, don't you know that Miles guy?"

The group turned to look at her, their eyes drifting to her hands. Holding the paper towels as if offering them to the universe, the wet towels dripped a small pool of water on the floor. "Uhm, yes I know Miles. "

Not wanting a re-enactment of the media frenzy of questions from her co-workers, she darted from the room hearing the tall intern ask what the deal was with the paper towels.

She returned to her desk and cleaned it like a white-glove inspection was scheduled at noon. To her surprise, the designers left her alone and didn't bombard her with questions. Her don't-bother-me mood was no doubt clear. Just to make it perfectly clear, when she started on her project design, she posted her confiscated hotel "Do Not Disturb" sign on her workstation wall.

Olivia wanted to get as much work done as possible. Something was telling her that she might need to take some time off soon.

SIXTEEN

⁓

Driving home, Olivia couldn't stop thinking about Miles. He had not looked his normal stylish self in the news conference earlier. She'd never seen that puffiness under his eyes. When had he gotten a full night's sleep last? His stress level must be off the charts.

Stopping by the corner grocery store in the Central West End, she picked up a bottle of nice wine and platter of cheese and crackers. An impromptu visit from a friend might be exactly what Miles needed.

He was usually the consummate host with his elegant dinner parties delighting guests with catered food, martinis, and a balcony view of the Cathedral Basilica of St. Louis. The Basilica – a draw for tourists and devoted Catholics featured one of the largest mosaic collections in the world. She'd also heard that the basement contained not just a museum, but crypts of cardinals and archbishops. The condo's second balcony, facing East from the master bedroom, had a sweet view of the Arch. Prime real estate.

The guest parking spot was open. She parked and grabbed the wine and platter. Walking around to the front of the three-story brick building, a neighbor leaving the building held the door for her. Luck was with her today. On the third floor, she knocked gently. No answer. Setting down the bottle of wine, she knocked less gently. And waited. So much for luck.

She grabbed her Blackberry from her purse and called him. Maybe he was still on his way home.

"Olivia?"

"Hey Miles. Will you be home soon?"

"I'm home now."

"Then why aren't you answering the door?"

"Oh my, is that you at the door?"

She heard the deadbolt unlock.

"Come in, my dear. I'm so sorry." He looked suspiciously into the hallway.

"Miles, are you ok? What's that all about?"

"The media has my address. They were waiting inside the hall at my condo door this morning. Trying to get a head start on their competitors before the scheduled news conference."

"The hallway door? Is that legal?"

"Good question. I need to tell my neighbors to avoid letting just anyone in."

"Geez Miles, this is crazy."

"Crazy is a small word, sweet pea."

Presenting the bottle of wine, Olivia soothed, "I've brought some appropriate medicine."

"Bless you, child." A faint smile drifted across his face.

Two glasses of wine, a couple napkins, some tiny white plates with their selected cheese and crackers, and they settled into the chenille couch. Olivia moved the luxurious pillows – the only ostrich-feather decorated pillows she'd ever seen.

Miles quickly sipped the wine a few times. Holding back her hundred questions, she waited for him to open the conversation. Half a plate of crackers and cheese later, he sighed. "I'm sure you saw the interviews."

"Interviews? It reminds me of that awful childhood game – bombardment... Why do guys like to play that anyway? It always left red marks on my legs when that nasty rubber ball hit me. One time I threw the ball at myself just to get out of the game. Everyone laughed. Except my gym teacher who made me do ten laps..."

"Olivia?"

"Oh, sorry, I'm getting off track."

"No, no. I just wanted to say how sweet it was for you to stop by."

She leaned across the couch and kissed his cheek. He held her a little longer than usual.

"Wow, you really are glad I stopped by," she teased.

"You're like my oasis right now, sweet pea."

Miles slowly released her and poured the second glass of wine. His weary face started to relax.

She touched his hand, "Are you going to be ok, sweetie?"

The normal Miles returned. He sat up a little straighter and pushed the hair back from his forehead, "Of course I will. This is just a minor annoyance."

"You're not worried about your career?"

"My career?"

"Sure. I mean, do you think the Museum will get nasty?"

"If you're asking will they fire me and use me as a scapegoat, the answer is not in a million years. That's an assumption of guilt. We just have to get through this media frenzy."

"It seems to be escalating."

"Considerably."

"Maybe after the autopsy report is completed, they'll settle down."

"That depends on what's in the report."

Olivia settled into the sofa. "How do you think the director died?"

"No clue."

"A guess?"

"No thanks. The Museum is buzzing about a possible heart attack since there's no clear sign how he died. No blood or signs of physical assault. Just dropped on the floor beside the exhibit as they were getting ready to unveil the faience."

She nodded politely. It just was not a good time to share with him that she'd slipped into the fundraiser the night the director died.

She sipped her wine. "What about the Egyptian curse?"

"Olivia," he admonished. "You do understand that's propaganda to try to stop the outflow of artifacts from Egypt."

"Well if it's just propaganda, then why is the media jumping on it?"

He raised his eyebrows, "Because it's propaganda, sweet pea."

"I'm sensing some animosity toward the media."

"Really? I can't imagine why."

The landline phone rang. He checked the caller ID and came back to the couch. "Speak of the devil."

"They don't let up, do they?"

"Not in their job description."

"Miles, do you think a sacrificial event would help?"

"Such as?"

"An unveiling of the faience?"

He sat back, rubbing his forehead.

"It would divert media attention from the director's murder," she proposed.

"Murder?"

"Well, let's say death then. And the Museum's patrons and the public would also be appeased if the media covered the faience unveiling. Plus Dr. Hasaneen would be reassured of its safety…"

"Maybe someone else would like to see it also?" he suggested.

"Who me? Oh. Well, of course, I'd be open to an invitation from a friend."

He laughed at her coyness.

"It makes a lot of sense, sweet pea. There's been quite a bit of talk about this at the Museum. Not that you heard this from me, but it's on the Board meeting agenda tomorrow."

"When do you think they would unveil it?"

"Soon."

She crunched a cracker to calm herself. "Were you serious about getting me an invitation if it happens?"

"For you, sweet pea, I can do this."

Her heart was racing too fast. What were the chances that she could keep her promise to Amro and stay away from the Museum?

Should she really be loyal to a guy she barely knew?

Maybe she was looking for an excuse.

Her Blackberry rang. She scrambled for her phone. It was Amro. Was this guy psychic? She remembered his words – *We're connected, Olivia.*

"Hey, can I call you back later? I'm at a friend's place?"

"Sure, Olivia. Everything ok?" His silky voice was making her blush.

"Of course."

"So you'll call me later then?" There was something irresistibly sexy about this exotic guy pursuing her so unabashedly.

"I will."

"Promise?"

She heard herself giggle. "Yes, I promise." As soon as the word promise came out of her mouth, she felt guilty about her excitement to attend the next unveiling. If Miles could arrange it. If she dared to go back again.

Maybe Jonathon was right when he teased her about being under the spell of the faience.

"Call me back Olivia. I'll be waiting for you."

When she hung up, she saw the grin on Miles face.

"Well now, who was that?"

She poured herself the rest of the wine. "No one."

"That no one is making you blush."

"That's just from the wine."

"Sure." Miles was not one to push.

She jumped up to refill their little white plates with crackers and cheese from the platter in the kitchen. "So Miles, really, I'm curious what you think … if the director was murdered, who do you think the culprit would be?"

"Probably the art dealer."

"Why?"

"To protect any information the director had about him."

"What do you think the director knew?"

Miles' shrug was less than convincing. He crossed his legs and let out a little yawn. "Do you mind if I call it a night?"

She could tell he was uncomfortable. He'd said more than he planned to. One thing she knew for sure about Miles, when the wall came down only time would bring it up again.

"You do look tired."

"So sorry, sweet pea."

"I understand." Their eyes locked, knowing that she understood more than his excuse of being tired.

SEVENTEEN

The next morning Olivia was late for work. A traffic jam had her stalled on the Forest Park Parkway. She'd never seen it completely stopped for so long. Flipping radio stations for a traffic report, she drummed her fingers on the steering wheel. As a native St. Louisan, she was unaccustomed to gridlock and had no patience for it. Friends in Washington D.C. shared the horrors of their beltway commutes... hours of bumper to bumper combat with crashes of colossal nature. Last week, she'd gotten an e-mail from one of her college buddies, Jill, telling her all the nitty-gritty details of an overturned semi that had catapulted up the side of a sound barrier wall taller than a one-story house. A little traffic in St. Louis paled in comparison. But still, she needed to get to work. Her creative director was probably already growling about her whereabouts.

The traffic report was finally on…

Reports coming in of a bad traffic jam on Forest Park Parkway. No accidents have been reported in the area. The jam is believed to be due to a large crowd of media enroute to the Art Museum to cover the recently deceased director's autopsy report.

The Museum has called a press conference for nine a.m. Looks like this may be the event of the decade here in St. Louis, Robin.

Thanks Terry. I think this may be the event of more than a decade though.

You're right Robin. Our traffic helicopter reporter is getting a glimpse of it now and says he's never seen anything like this.

I can tell you our reporters are having a real hard time getting to the Museum. Any way the traffic helicopter could land a few of them on the roof or nearby Terry?

I think there would be some regulations that might be in the way. Not to mention all those trees in Forest Park surrounding the Museum.

Right you are on that Robin.

Well for all you folks sitting in traffic, you might as well call in to work and let them know you'll be late. Really late.

Thanks Terry, we'll check back with you.

Olivia called in to work, left a message on her boss' voicemail, and called her friend Lisa to see if she could give her a play-by-play on any live news.

"Olivia! Where have you been, I haven't heard from you for so long? How'd the date go?"

The date? A few seconds went by before she remembered telling Lisa that she was getting ready for a "date" when she needed her help shopping on the cheap for a classy outfit for her meeting with the Museum staffer. The outfit was perfect for convincing the young staffer that she was the daughter of a distinguished art collector.

"Oh, the date? Just ok. No chemistry."

"Bummer. Well I know your soul mate is out there, Olivia. Just before I met my husband, I'd totally given up and then we literally bumped into each other in the produce aisle. How corny is that?"

Olivia managed not to sigh. She'd heard this story so many times. But she knew Lisa loved to tell it. It was her inspirational story for her lone single friend.

"Hey Lisa... I'm in a nasty traffic jam on Forest Park Parkway..."

"That's weird. It doesn't usually get backed up."

"I know. And my boss is gonna be really mad. Can you check to see if there's anything on the television about this?"

"Sure. Let me switch over from the cartoons. Don't be surprised if you hear some crying in the background.

My son wails if I dare change the cartoon channel." Sure
enough, there was an immediate wail when the sound of
the news came on. "Wow, there's something crazy going
on at the Museum. Hold on... I'll turn it up... Something
about an autopsy report from the director who died.
Honey, can you stop crying for a second, I can't hear.
Here, play with the baby bear. Big hugs for bear..."

Olivia was accustomed to the dual conversation and
knew Lisa wasn't asking her to hug the bear. But she
really wanted to know what the news was saying. "Lisa...
what are they saying?"

"Let me turn it up more... Wow! I can't believe it!"

Olivia waited. This could simply mean that Lisa's
toddler had stopped crying and was hugging the bear.

"CNN is reporting on the front steps of the Art
Museum. They just said that the autopsy report says that
the director's death is ruled probable homicide. Poison
was found in his system! Something about a fast acting
poison that constricted the airways allowing no sound.
Wow, I've never seen so much media... they're doing
a helicopter view now. Honey, don't put that in your
mouth. Give it to Mommie. Sorry Olivia, I have to go,
my son is eating my wedding picture frame..."

"I understand. Thanks for checking."

Probable homicide. Now she felt like joining Lisa's
son in his wailing.

110

She stared straight ahead at the line of crawling traffic. The excitement of the Egyptian treasure, meeting an exotic new man, trying to get a sneak view of the faience, had filled her with adrenalin. But homicide changed the excitement to a chilling shock.

This was no longer a fun game… an escape from her normal routine and yearning for more in her life.

The director had been murdered the night she was at the Museum. The night she met Amro and was whisked away in her hired limo with the help of his friend, the museum guard. The night she used a false identity to get into an exclusive fundraiser so she could see the faience.

Her fingers no longer drummed on the steering wheel. The traffic jam suddenly was not important.

EIGHTEEN

Two hours late for work. A new record for traffic jams in St. Louis. Fortunately, her creative director was in the same traffic. His layers of expletives were heard throughout the hallway when he arrived.

Another traffic jam was in the agency break room. The television was surrounded like the twelfth Krispy Kreme donut in a staff meeting of thirteen. This was the biggest news to hit St. Louis that Olivia remembered and the agency staff wasn't about to let work get in the way of the play-by-play on it. Even a senior vice president was part of the cluster.

CNN was rehashing what Lisa had told her from the earlier news – probable homicide from poisoning. Olivia joined the group, watching numbly. It was just too much to absorb.

Sharon, the agency resident dramatist, caught her shaking her head and buddied up beside her, "This is some crazy shit isn't it?"

Olivia shook her head in agreement.

"So are you gonna get the scoop from your Museum friends on who they think murdered the dude?"

"Sharon, I don't think my friends are interested in talking about this right now."

"Oh, well excuse me. It's not like it won't be all over the news soon. The cops are gonna be crawling all over that place." Her eyes lit up as she thought of another escalation. "I'll bet this will be one of those FBI cases since it's such a big stinking deal. I mean, we've got media swarming the Museum like a frigging hostage takedown."

"You've been watching too many movies Sharon."

"Honey, this is a movie. Oh, check that out, it's that Egyptian expert guy. He's kinda hot for an old guy." She jumped up closer to the television that was barely visible for all the standing bodies surrounding it.

Dr. Hasaneen had traveled to St. Louis and now stood on the top step of the Museum front entrance like it was his domain. Reporters raced toward him. The

Museum public relations team, which had been fielding questions, was abandoned.

Completely calm, Dr. Hasaneen waited for all the reporters to gather around him and listened in silence to their litany of questions. Dressed in a simple blue jean shirt and khaki's, he contrasted with the Museum's public relations team in crisp suits and white shirts.

The team, although perfectly attired, was visually unnerved by the media's pressure to learn more, to find an immediate answer to who murdered the director.

Dr. Hasaneen looked only slightly ruffled in attire, likely from an overnight trip from Cairo. But his calm presence was unshakable. Raising one hand in the air, he silenced the frenzied reporters. Like a concert pianist holding his hands over the keys in a dramatic pause, the esteemed archeologist cleared his throat, "Today is a significant moment in history. It is a moment when I come here to this Museum, a museum that has had a strong and respectable presence, to ask that the right thing be done.

King Tutankhamun was a pharaoh known through-out the world for his young reign and questionable death. When he died at just 18 years of age, his tomb was filled with treasures and mostly spared the plundering of the tombs of many other pharaohs. But we have never been able to find the tomb of his young mother, a second wife who may have been buried less exquisitely.

Now, we have finally found an artifact connected with the young King's mother. As King Tutankhamun's tour of museums comes to a close, we embrace his upcoming return to Egypt where he can rest and enjoy his rightful eternity.

But the young King died in a manner that may have been traumatic when he was just 18 years old. Although ruling as a king, he was still bridging the time between boy and man. A boy who would miss his mother and want her by his side.

And now, a part of his mother's grave, the faience, is no longer where it belongs. This is a disturbance of destiny. A disturbance of a son's right to know that his mother is respected and properly cared for in her burial.

So we are here today on this unusual moment of an autopsy report of the director of this important Museum. An autopsy report that signifies his death as a probable murder. Should this be by hands of man or hands of nature, the destiny is the same. This is the Egyptian curse that befalls tomb raiders.

The only way to stop the curse is to return the faience to Egypt. This is why I am here today. To stop this curse from continuing and affecting those who have a part in this tomb raiding. And to bring the faience back to the rightful place so that King Tutankhamun can rest with his mother's artifact rightfully returned."

He paused, looking out over the tree-lined pond toward the cityscape of the Arch and a clear blue sky. An odd sound of thunder disturbed the crowd of reporters; several looked up curiously into the clear sky.

The media stared at Dr. Hasaneen in a rare hushed moment.

"I go now to meet with the Museum's leaders."

Before they could wind up their questions, he had disappeared into the double doors opened widely for him by the Museum guards.

In the agency break room another rare hush had descended.

Sharon handled that in her usual style, "Holy shit, that guy is like some kinda pharaoh himself." Her throaty smoker's-laced laughter ricocheted. As was often the case, she had a way of clearing a room. This was one of those cases.

After completing the cover design of an exhibitor's kit for one of their association clients in Washington D.C., her thoughts drifted back to the Museum. She wondered if Amro had heard that Dr. Hasaneen was in St. Louis. And was a little surprised that he hadn't texted her. News at this level was hard to miss if you were anywhere near St. Louis.

She sent him a quick text – *Did you hear that Dr. Hasaneen is in St. Louis?*

Fifteen minutes later he still hadn't texted back. She shrugged it off and went back to working on the interior pages, the sell sheets, of the exhibitor kit.

By the end of the day she still hadn't received a text from Amro.

On the way home, she called him. No answer. She left a message.

Where was he?

A little worried, a little ticked, she stopped for a rare drive-thru dinner – McDonald's fries and fish sandwich, no tartar sauce. Not that she was thinking about her diet today. She just didn't like tartar sauce.

Back at the apartment, she woofed it down and then had the delayed guilt about the fat grams and lack of nutrition. So she brooded.

Why did this guy seem so interested and then just ignore her?

Why was she even allowing this guy, who she knew so little about, affect her life?

If this kept up, he would also negatively affect her waistline.

The phone rang. She jumped up and grabbed it before the third ring.

"Hey Liv, did you make it home through all the awful traffic?"

"Oh, Jonathon. Yes, I'm home."

"Wow, that was not very enthusiastic. Were you expecting a phone call from someone else?"

"No, no…"

"Liv, are you keeping something from me? A new guy in your life?"

"It's not that. I just succumbed to McDonald's drive-thru and feel like I should do the Rosary or something."

"I thought you were Jewish?"

"I am. But my father's side is Catholic. My step-dad was Jewish though. Sometimes you have to cover all your bases."

"That's right. Your step-dad adopted you and gave you his last name."

"Yes, there aren't too many part Jewish and Catholic girls with the name Katz. Perhaps a few though."

"Love it," he chuckled. "Now back to the Rosary. Tell me what you're feeling nervous about."

"I'm worried about Miles."

"You mean because of all this crazy news about the autopsy report and Dr. Hasaneen being at the Museum?"

"You heard?"

"Honey, I'm living this one. The Museum was a zoo today."

Olivia burst out laughing. Maybe it was her stress level or just the silliness of what he said, but it was minutes before she could contain herself.

"Was it really that funny?"

"Yes." Olivia declared, wiping her tears.

"Well get ready for some more laughs then because word is that Dr. Hasaneen isn't leaving St. Louis anytime soon."

"Oh?"

"Nope. He's demanding that the faience be shown to him before he leaves."

"Will the Museum do that?"

"He managed to get a private meeting with the board chair and Miles today. At the Board meeting this afternoon a vote was taken and it will be announced tomorrow to the media that a brief showing of the faience exhibit will take place for the Egyptian archeologist and a select group."

"Who's going to be in the select group?"

"Our Egyptian exhibit benefactors, a few top donors, and a short list of media from what I hear."

"Jonathon, is there any way…"

"You can't possibly be about to ask me if I can get you in?"

"Well I just wondered if…"

"Liv, you really are completely under a spell. Do you want to be considered a suspect?"

"No, absolutely not. But maybe I could be somewhere where I wouldn't be seen."

"Perhaps behind the curtains of the opera balcony?" He chided.

"Come on, Jonathon."

"Seriously Liv. I know how badly you want to see the faience. But it just wouldn't make sense considering your attendance at the previous botched unveiling."

"Maybe I could design a media pass…"

"Liv! Clear your head on this one. Security will be extra tight. I've heard that they're bringing in extra contract security even."

She sighed. "You're right."

"Well, I'm glad you see that."

"So what night will the brief exhibit take place?"

NINETEEN

Since Jonathon refused to divulge the day of the faience unveiling, Olivia dropped by the local newsstand the next morning.

Omar, who knew his customers well, reached for the daily *St. Louis Sun Journal.* He smiled warmly, and she found herself returning the predictable but welcomed exchange.

Two blocks later she was back at her apartment ready to sift through the paper for details. It was a quick sift since the ongoing Museum story was front-page news again.

Museum Submits to Egyptian Demands

St. Louis, Missouri – The St. Louis Museum will hold a brief exhibit of the infamous Egyptian artifact declared to be from the tomb of King Tutankhamun. Dr. Hasaneen, head of Egyptian antiquities, demanded that he and the public have a viewing of the faience to ensure that it is safe.

The faience was previously scheduled to be unveiled at a private museum event. That unveiling was interrupted by the death of the museum director who died beside the empty exhibit case. Guests were stunned to see his body on the marble museum floor. An autopsy report released yesterday stated the death as a probable homicide.

Dr. Hasaneen arrived in St. Louis yesterday from Cairo with a fervent declaration that the faience must be returned to its homeland. He claims that the museum director is considered a tomb raider and has died from the historical Egyptian curse.

The museum stated that they do not agree with the archeologist regarding the Egyptian curse, but they are willing to exhibit the faience to reassure the public that it is safe and in good condition.

The private brief exhibit will take place Monday evening when the museum is closed. The exhibit will not be open to the public.

So Monday it was. Olivia wondered if she dared attend. Her heart jumped just thinking of it… actually seeing the beautiful faience with the turquoise blue lotus flowers and the earthy clay. She imagined the young King's mother holding the bowl, absorbing the beauty of it in her hands.

And she thought about the artist who made the faience. What would he have thought about this international frenzy regarding his ancient bowl? Could he have even imagined a time when the world would be so connected that a bowl could be discovered a continent away?

The artist in Olivia felt proud that his work was receiving such acclaim. But she was also realistic and knew that it was less about the artist and more about the pharaohs, the royal families, and repatriation or a country's right to retrieve their art when it goes missing.

The thought of seeing the faience was heavy on her mind. She'd have to decide quickly whether or not she was going to slip into the exhibit Monday night.

It was going to be a long weekend. And to make matters worse, she still hadn't heard from Amro. Her frustration with him was building.

Was he involved with someone? Did he go somewhere?

She stopped herself from the endless what ifs. She needed to concentrate on the decision at hand - to attend or not attend the exhibit.

Over the weekend she imagined being at the exhibit when she wasn't distracted about Amro.

At seven a.m. her Blackberry rang and vibrated on her nightstand. Patting for it, eyes half closed, she answered sleepily. "Hello?"

"Good Monday morning Liv. This is your reminder call."

"Jonathon?"

He laughed. "You really aren't a morning person."

"What reminder?"

"The reminder to not try anything silly tonight. Like just happening to drop by the Museum tonight for the exhibit."

"How'd you know that I knew it's tonight..."

"Omar said you picked up a paper this weekend."

"You've been checking on me!"

"Only because I love you. This is serious Liv. Really serious. I just don't think you understand that you could be a suspect here."

"You really think so?"

An exasperated sigh forced her to hold the Blackberry away from her ear. "Yes, yes, and yes!"

"Ok, I understand."

"Do you promise to *not* come to the Museum tonight?"

"Jonathon!"

"I want a promise."

"Fine, I promise."

"If it makes you feel any better, I heard that Channel 5 will be covering the event live. So you can watch it at ten o'clock."

"My place or yours?"

"It will have to be yours and solo. The Museum needs me to help out tonight. All hands on deck it seems."

"Keep an eye on Miles. I'm still worried about him."

"Me too."

"I'm headed to the Museum now. Remember your promise."

"Yes sir."

"You're so cute when you don't get your way."

———

After one of the longest days at the office, she stopped for a famous St. Louis style pizza. The multi-cheese concoction was an acquired taste. Friends from other cities were struck by the unusual taste, having had more of a mozzarella-only experience. She reminded them that St. Louis had originated the ice cream cone and hot dog during the World's Fair in 1904 held in Forest Park. Since then other striking, but more localized food, had become St. Louis favorites like toasted ravioli, a toasty fried version dipped in marinara sauce, and gooey butter cake, a sweet and tart lemony cake sprinkled with powdered sugar. The toasted ravioli had been a hit with her friend Jill from Washington D.C., but the gooey butter cake had caused her face to pinch into a dramatic corkscrew.

Two hours later Olivia, in her comfy sweats, was curled up on the couch beside her coffee table that displayed an opened pizza box missing half of its slices. Pizza, her nemesis and buddy, was her food weakness and the primary culprit for her extra ten pounds or so.

One hour to go before the late news. She switched from HGTV to Channel 5 ready to catch any early news teases. The first tease came during the commercial break from the hospital drama programming.

Standing outside of the Museum the senior female broadcaster, who had been delivering news to the community for more than twenty-five years, was dressed in a stunning ivory suit likely provided by Neiman's. This story was a career pinnacle no doubt. It was not a stretch to say that the world would be watching this on the satellite feeds.

Tonight at 10 we'll have the most exciting unveiling in St. Louis' history – live coverage of the now infamous Egyptian artifact. The Museum director's recent murder has been linked to the Egyptian curse for his role in the artifact's suspicious procurement. Join us at 10 for live coverage of the private museum unveiling.

Olivia was properly teased. Her heart rate had increased and she regretted not sneaking into the exhibit tonight. When would she ever have a chance to see the faience in person? What if the faience was returned to Egypt or just kept under lock and key?

She stretched out on the couch and dreamed about being at the unveiling.

Forty minutes later, she awoke with a sharp jump. The cable box clock read 9:55 p.m. Shaking her head at her near miss of the news story, she grabbed the remote and turned up the volume. The results of last night's sleep deprivation and half a box of pizza were more powerful than she anticipated.

The hospital drama had just ended and the news started.

The veteran broadcaster in her elegant suit was inside the Museum. A small, hushed group stood near a table of ignored hors d'ouevres. The excitement had squashed appetites. Two other media groups – CNN and BBC – were visible in the background.

BBC was in a whispered interview with Dr. Hasaneen.

CNN had Miles cornered.

Channel 5 positioned themselves with Dr. Jacobs, the Art Museum board chair. "Dr. Jacobs, we understand that you're about to unveil the now infamous Egyptian artifact. Can you tell us if you've seen it yourself today?"

"Candice, I'm about to go now and check on the faience before we unveil it."

"Is it behind the curtain in the new Egyptian Exhibit area?"

"Yes."

"Can you tell our viewers, Dr. Jacobs, what the Museum's take is on Dr. Hasaneen's assertions that the faience should be returned to Cairo?"

"We certainly appreciate Dr. Hasaneen's perspective. However, we stand by our procurement and have every intention of keeping the faience here in St. Louis."

"And do you believe that the Egyptian curse is behind the Museum director's recent murder?"

"Candice, we don't prescribe to this folklore."

"How is the Museum feeling about Dr. Schneider's death?"

"We're deeply saddened. Very deeply saddened."

"Understandable. Are there any suspicions about who might have wanted the director dead?"

"Not at all. We're leaving this in the hands of law enforcement to handle."

"Is this being handled by local police or FBI?"

"I'm really not at liberty to say, Candice. Now if you'd be so kind to pardon me, I need to check on the faience and prepare for the unveiling."

"Of course. Thank you for your time, Dr. Jacobs."

He slipped behind the curtain, once again draped in silk from column to column at the entry of the Egyptian Exhibit.

The crowd of less than thirty media, benefactors, and dignitaries tensed with anticipation as the board chair disappeared behind the curtain. Olivia switched to lotus position, her eyes trained on the television screen at an intensity beyond any Superbowl or Olympic event. In just a few minutes, the faience would be shown.

Candice continued her background story as they waited. From the wider shot they had switched to, Olivia could see that security had increased. A few of them had the look of contracted off-duty cops. Amongst them, Olivia saw the guard who had ferreted her and Amro out of the Museum when the director was murdered. He joined the cops in their small talk.

The minutes dragged by, apparently for the media also.

"We're not sure what's taking so long. But we're committed to staying live during our wait."

Miles had finally disengaged from CNN only to be captured by Channel 5.

"Excuse me, you're the curator Miles Sanders, correct?"

"Yes, that's correct."

"Can you tell us what the delay is about?"

"It may just be a transport issue. We want to be very careful of course."

"Of course. Can you tell us when our viewers can expect to see the Egyptian artifact though?"

"Actually, I'm headed over there now to check on it."

"Great. We'll stand by then. Meanwhile, we'll continue to share with our viewers more history on the young King's reign."

Miles nodded and walked out of camera range.

Moments later, Olivia recognized his voice heard from the news live shot. "Oh dear god, no!"

Olivia gasped. Channel 5, BBC, and CNN dashed toward the curtain before the guards could stop them. The camera showed the back of Candice in a run toward the curtain that had dropped from the media onslaught.

Just before the guards pushed the media back, there was a glimpse of Dr. Jacobs' fallen body beside the empty faience exhibit case. Miles was bent over him, looking up at the group in dismay.

The board chair appeared to be dead.

TWENTY

If Olivia thought she was sleep deprived the night before, it paled to the two hours of sleep she got after the live news showed Dr. Jacobs' limp body beside the empty faience exhibit.

Her mind raced all night. Where was the faience? Who wanted to kill Dr. Jacobs? Was it the same person who had killed the Museum director? How could both the director and board chair end up dead the exact same way? Was this the curse or a serial murder? Where was Amro?

She tried calling him repeatedly last night, completely disregarding her pride or following any rules on number of calls that any reasonable person would make within a few hours. But she only got his voicemail.

Was he beginning to feel the heat of being on a suspect list of those who attended the fundraiser when Dr. Schneider was killed?

What if he was beginning to be suspicious about her?

After all, they really didn't know each other. The circumstances had thrown them together and forced them to form an alliance.

Should she be suspicious of him?

And so her mind traversed throughout the inky black night. The questions representing an endless number of sheep blocking her from sleep.

———————

She was really cranky when she got to the office.

The television patrol of agency employees and interns hovered in the break room. A near Mardi Gras atmosphere penetrated the room as the macabre crowd discussed the homicides and exchanged hypotheses on the murderer. There was a strong division between those who believed in a motive-induced murderer and those who believed in the Egyptian curse. When their voices rose in a fevered pitch about who would be next, Olivia left the room.

It was all too clear. The next person with a large target on his chest was her beloved Miles.

The vibration of her Blackberry in her pocket made her jump. She grabbed it, expecting that Amro was finally returning her onslaught of calls. It was Jonathon.

"Olivia?" He was surprised that she answered – a rare moment in her work ethic crazed behavior.

"Jonathon?"

"You answered. Are you at the office?"

"Yes."

"You saw the news last night."

"Yes."

"Can you meet me at my place this evening?"

"Yes."

"I'm too stunned right now to make a crack about how many times you've just said yes. So let's try for one more… Meet me at seven?"

"Ok."

He exhaled a half chuckle at her non-compliance. "See you then Liv."

They clicked off. No need to discuss the reasons.

Olivia went to her desk and plowed through her endless assignments. She felt an increasing level of anxiousness … about what might happen to Miles next.

Promptly at seven Olivia buzzed into Jonathon's condo building. As usual his door was ajar welcoming her after her three-flight climb. Two glasses of cabernet and a tray of cheese, hummus, and crackers drew her to the mahogany coffee table.

"I'm just changing clothes Liv. Be right there."

The beautifully appointed condo always looked like a magazine photographer was on his way over to shoot a home design cover. The only imperfection was the ghastly heat since Jonathon was so opposed to AC. Fortunately, she'd stopped at her dusty apartment and changed into jogging shorts and a 100% cotton t-shirt. A close match to Jonathon's attire she noticed when he appeared from the bedroom.

"You changed also! So smart you are," he grinned. Their battles about AC had been ongoing for five years. The only place she lost this battle was in his condo. "Do you think the platter is enough food or should we order a pizza?"

"No pizza, please. I devoured half a box last night."

"Very well then. Parisian-style tonight. The wine will fill us up." He offered her a glass and tapped it with his. "Santé."

"To Miles' safety." She tapped her glass against his.

"Absolutely. To Miles' safety."

They both took a long sip. Jonathon swung his arm in a long curve inviting her to the couch. It was time to talk business.

"So is the Museum in a near panic at this point?"

"Panic seems like a mild word."

"What's everyone saying? Do they think it's the Egyptian curse or a murderer?"

"It's like the continental divide."

"It's the same at the agency."

"Some people are completely opposed to considering something mystical. But those who believe in the curse are completely convinced."

"And what side are you on Jonathon?"

He topped off her glass of wine and refilled his. Taking a sip, he smoothed his hair back from his forehead followed up by a short sigh. He circled the top of his wine glass with his index finger.

"What side Jonathon?"

Darting a glance at her direct stare, he jumped up from the couch and walked to the window that over-looked the condo courtyard. "Miles is completely opposed to the idea of a curse. He calls it folklore."

"That's Miles' opinion then. Did you tell him that you're on the opposing side?

He returned to the couch, a frown lined his forehead. When he looked up, his blue eyes were as honest as a young child. "We've talked about this before Liv. And yes, I think it's the Egyptian curse."

She nodded. It wasn't easy for a grown man with a doctorate degree to confirm that he believed in what many of his colleagues referred to as folklore. Reaching for his hand, she held it with resolve. "I believe you're right."

"This is so crazy Liv."

"Do you think there's any way to convince Miles that it is a curse?"

"Never."

"That's what I was afraid of."

"He's already changed his phone to an unlisted number and plans on staying with friends for a few weeks rather than live in his condo. Miles knows he's the next target. But he thinks it's from a person who murdered the director and now the board chair."

"Glad to hear that he's taking precautions. That gives us more time."

"More time?"

"Yes. You do realize we have to devise a plan to reverse this curse?"

"What are you talking about Liv?"

"The only way to keep Miles alive is to reverse the curse."

"How the hell would someone reverse the curse?"

She stared at him, shocked that he did not see the clear solution.

"Jonathon, the faience has to be returned to Egypt."

TWENTY-ONE

Olivia left Jonathon's apartment an hour later. He was too stunned to move forward with any planning tonight. She would give him a little time. But with time being their enemy, she could only give him until tomorrow.

Her Blackberry rang. Amro, at last!

"Where have you been?"

"Olivia, please don't be upset."

"I tried calling you about a hundred times."

"This is why I'm calling you just as soon as I've come back."

"Back? From where?"

"Let's talk in person. I need to see your lovely face. Are you anywhere near the Starbucks by your place?"

"Yes, just a block away actually."

"Perfect. I'm there now."

She looked down at her jogging shorts and comfy t-shirt. "I need to drop something off at my apartment first. See you in fifteen minutes."

"For you Olivia, I would wait any amount of time."

This guy is good, she thought as she rushed to her apartment and changed into a perfect-fitting pair of jeans and a silk top. Part of her felt that she should not put out the extra effort for this guy. Still, she had to admit he was just that irresistible. Although she was determined to stay ahead of his game and resist him. But there was more to it. She felt connected to him.

And she had a strong feeling that she might need him in the future.

Rushing through the Starbucks door, perhaps a bit too fast, she spotted him instantly. He was sitting at the same table as when they had met before. His eyes rose from his glass of iced water and locked with hers.

Careful Olivia, her intuition told her in the voice of her Cherokee grandmother.

"Olivia! Come, sit with me." Amro pulled a chair back for her.

She sat. And tried to regain her composure.

"Can I get you a cappuccino?"

"Yes, that would be nice."

He disappeared around the partial wall to order her cappuccino. A few minutes later, when her breathing finally normalized again, he returned with her cappuccino in a special-order white mug.

She sipped the luscious foam. He watched.

Feeling as nervous as a first-day high school freshman, she couldn't bring herself to look at his eyes again.

He touched her hand, rippling a current throughout her body. "You look especially beautiful tonight. It's so good to be back."

Clearing her throat, she remembered the sleepless nights wondering where this guy was. "Where are you back from?"

"Cairo."

She lost her silly case of nervousness. "Cairo? Why didn't you say you were going to Cairo? I mean, you know we're not dating or anything and you don't owe me an explanation. But Amro we're in the middle of this whole crazy thing and it's gotten worse. Much worse."

"Worse? What's happened?"

"Amro, how could you not know? It's international news."

"I literally just left the airport and have been flying back and forth to Cairo…"

"So you don't know about the board chair of the art museum?"

"Know what Olivia?"

"He's been murdered."

He coughed on his ice water. Blotting the napkin over his lips, he tried to restore his flawless composure. "You can't be serious."

"Absolutely serious."

"When did this happen?"

"Monday. They were going to unveil the faience just like before. Dr. Hasaneen was there along with a short list of muckety-mucks and top media. When they checked to see where the faience was, they found his dead body exactly in the same area as the director."

"Was the faience there?"

"No. It had not been transported."

"Unbelievable." He sat back and rubbed his forehead. "Olivia, this is not good."

"I know. Believe me, I know."

"The curse is getting stronger. It's hard to say what will happen next. Anyone connected to this is in the eye of the curse."

The goose bumps that crept up her arms were not from the AC. Hearing his words brought reality to the situation. Reality was what she needed right now. Although she might need Amro in the future, the practical side nagged for details before she made herself more vulnerable.

"Amro, why were you in Cairo?"

"It was very sudden. My brother had an awful car accident."

She felt guilty for her cross-examination. "I'm so sorry. Is he ok?"

"He's recuperating."

"Nothing permanent I hope."

"Several broken bones and a collapsed lung. But he's expected to fully recuperate. He was very lucky."

She noticed that her hand had reached out and curled into the warmth of his golden brown hand. He stroked the back of her hand with his thumb. She was breathing too heavy again.

"Olivia, could we talk somewhere other than this noisy coffee shop?"

What was he asking for, she wondered. Did he want to come back to her apartment? If he did, could she resist him? The chemistry between them was like a silk curtain softly draping around them...

"Would you mind just taking a walk?"

"Oh, sure." Was that relief in her voice or disappointment?

The humid air gathered them into the night. A steady stream of cars circled as drivers searched for the rare open parking spot in the Central West End hub. Clusters of college students laughed and talked loudly in a pursuit for attention. A middle-aged couple, encircled in each other's half embrace, walked out of one of the restaurants, the earthy scent of Bordeaux trailed behind them.

Amro reached for her hand as they walked down a quieter block. He slowed the pace at a gated residential area. Against the curve of the dark wrought iron, he cupped the top of her hip in his hand and pressed her gently against the gate.

"Is your apartment nearby?"

"Yes," she heard herself whisper through her fog.

As they walked the four blocks her Grandmother's voice came to her again … Be careful. She regained her composure and stopped. "Amro, this is too fast for me. I hope you understand." She didn't want to send him away rejected.

"I respect that Olivia. But I will walk you to your apartment to make sure you're safe."

It was enticing to feel that he was protecting her.

But did he think that she was in danger?

TWENTY-TWO

To her surprise she slept safe and sound. Amro had that effect on her ... made her feel safe. It was a strange combination, both enticing and confusing.

The chirp of her Blackberry pulled her away from her thoughts. She ran to her bedroom nightstand where she always kept it. But it wasn't there. Thinking of Amro last night had her so distracted she had left it in her bag. She smiled and ran into the living room, grabbed her bag, and read the text from Jonathon.

Twenty minutes later, she was showered, dressed, and eating a breakfast bar as she headed out the door to Jonathon's place. He was ready to talk about "the return."

His condo smelled of glorious freshly brewed coffee. He handed her a cup without pretense. She sighed as the caffeine soaked in. Without asking, he accepted her empty cup, refilled it with the perfect blend of milk and honey, and handed it off to her again.

"Did you call in sick this morning?"

"Yes. You too?"

Jonathon nodded affirmatively. "You look a little flushed."

"Just rushed over here, I guess."

"Hope I wasn't interrupting anything?"

"Jonathon! Are you my chaperone now?"

He smiled at her defensiveness. "Not at all. Just a doting friend. But you can tell me when you're ready, honey."

"Can we talk about the faience?"

"Yes, of course. God help us."

"Some divine inspiration would be helpful…"

As they talked about returning the faience back to Egypt, the sun rose to a noontime peak. Jonathon gathered a tray of turkey cold cuts, fresh sourdough bread, and provolone cheese from his ever supplied kitchen. They moved to the patio overlooking the manicured courtyard and talked in hushed tones that dropped to silence when a neighbor passed along the sidewalk leading to the entrance. By two o'clock, they needed a stretch and walked to Starbucks for cappuccinos. Walking throughout the Central West End, sipping cappuccino, they laced arms feeling a bond beyond their years of friendship. The combination of linking together, to save Miles and to be catalysts in a rare act of repatriation in the art world, brought a new level to their comradery. As the sun drifted behind the buildings, they headed back to his condo with the initial plan.

In the Japanese maple ahead a crow screeched.

She knew Jonathon would do anything to protect her.

But what was she getting him into?

It was the highest risk either had ever taken.

This plan not only put their careers at stake, it would potentially land them in prison. Or the graveyard.

TWENTY-THREE

~~~~~~~~~~

Research had been her weakness in college. Now Jonathon had assigned her a research project. In college poor research could mean a poor grade. It was far worse in this assignment – a failure of research could mean her life would be at risk.

And her research was on an unknown stopwatch. Now that the curse was hanging over Miles' head. His life could be in jeopardy at any time.

The history museum library was separated from the main museum by just over a mile. Tucked along the west side of Forest Park, most St. Louisans were unfamiliar with this low-profile little gem with just a few stingy parking spots and signage that only those with tenacity and crisp vision would find.

Olivia arrived at noon during her lunch break. The library had hours even bankers from days gone by could dream of – noon to five with the exception of Saturday, ten to five. She had beat the crowd though and found a parking spot.

With only an hour to escape from work before it was noticeable, she felt like an ER trauma surgeon. This was a golden hour for her future and Miles' safety.

Turning the door handle, she jolted at the locked door.

There was no time for this. She knocked. No answer. Circling around to the parking lot, she confirmed that there was another car in the lot. The late model Subaru was parked two spots from her car.

"Hello?" a faint voice called from the front of the library.

She rushed around the building, startling the white-haired gentleman standing at the front door as if it were his home. "Are you open?"

"Yes, dear. It's just now noon."

"I'm sorry, it's just that I'm on my lunch hour and have a lot of research to do…" she stepped past him into the cool conservatory of dusty books. She had been here once before and remembered the striking mosaics that curved up the convex ceiling. The rich wood tables and stacks of rare books pointed to a generous supply of benefactors. She sneezed.

"Bless you."

Dusty books wreaked havoc with her allergies. She rummaged for a Zyrtec in her purse.

"What are you looking for dear?"

"My allergy pill…"

She looked up when he cleared his throat.

"Oh. You mean here?"

"Yes, dear."

Why did these stuffy research places completely undo her? Bad memories she guessed. And this gentleman, although quite pleasant, was making her feel like a child asking her grandpa for chewing gum. Time to put her insecurities away.

"I need to research the tunnels underneath the city of St. Louis."

"Yes?"

"Well, it's for a research paper I'm working on for my Master's thesis."

"I hope you have more than an hour for this, my dear. We have many books about St. Louis architecture and the tunnels."

Fifteen long minutes later, he had extracted three books for her to take to a reading room. She grabbed the books and headed toward the room.

"Miss? One moment. You'll need to sign the guest book first and provide a photo ID."

What a lovely trail that would leave. He would probably log which books she took to the reading room. She pretended to search for her wallet. "I'm sorry, but I think I left my wallet at work today."

"That's quite alright." He waltzed over to her, lifted the books from her arms, and returned to his post behind the counter. "You can take these to the reading room tomorrow. When you remember your ID."

Hardball so soon. She couldn't help but admire this unflappable man defending this valuable property. In a sense similar to how Jonathon and she were defending the faience.

She decided to risk the possibility of the trail. Why shouldn't she have an interest in St. Louis architecture and its historical tunnels? It could relate to her design work.

Five minutes later, he had confiscated her driver's license and her purse. No purses, bookbags, or personal items were allowed in the reading rooms. Next time, she would lock her purse in her trunk. There simply was not time for all this process.

In the reading room, she looked up at the clock. Thirty minutes past the hour. Impossible.

She scanned the books contents and indexes searching for tunnels. The first book had a lengthy history about the tunnels. St. Louis was constructed upon a complex system of natural caves which had been converted to a spider-web of tunnels used for utility lines – 17 miles of steam tunnels, 200 miles of gas lines, 1,200 miles of underground water lines, 600 miles of electrical lines, and 10,000 miles of metropolitan sewer department water and waste systems. The tunnels were once used to transport goods, to hide arms and ammunition during the Civil War, as a burial repository for victims during the cholera epidemic of the mid-1800's, for underground storage for ice and perishables especially during the tropical summers, and for the German beer brewers that helped build the city to the fourth largest metropolitan city in the nation in 1904.

The brewers constructed stone arches, brick ceilings, staircases, walkways, and paved the floors – an elegant home for massive wooden kegs where the beer aged. Beer gardens and taverns in the caves became a cozy place to sell beer and entertain.

Prohibition and more recent auto and aviation manufacturing declines had stifled the city's growth, leaving it to hover around the fourteenth largest metropolitan area after a century passed.

Olivia was a little sad that her city had experienced this decline. Still she felt that with its growing markets in healthcare, education, and science, St. Louis had a lot of potential. Transitions were never easy.

She read on about a tunnel that she had heard once existed, but thought it was folklore – Cherokee Cave. The cave had been owned by one of the great brewery families – the Lemp family. Accessible from the spider-web of tunnels under the city and from the Lemp Mansion, the home and the cave were considered to be one of the most haunted areas in the nation.

Cherokee Cave stories about its haunted atmosphere included strange shapes and sounds heard in the cave. The story told was that a tormented Native American couple chose to die in the cave rather than be separated. The Cherokee girl was promised to a prominent member of her tribe rather than to the Sioux man who had captured her heart. So the deeply in love couple were forbidden to marry. The hauntings of their spirits, meant to push away intruders, allowed the couple to stay together in eternity.

This cave later housed the Lemp family's brewery business and also an elaborate entertainment area – an auditorium, ballroom, and swimming pool. The demise of the Lemp empire was considered a great mercantile tragedy of St. Louis. John Adam Lemp built a beer dynasty and died a millionaire.

The family was doing quite well until they purchased the elegant mansion above the Cherokee Cave. The heir apparent son mysteriously died. Three years later and still grieving for his favorite son, his father shot himself in one of the mansion's bedrooms.

Prohibition then destroyed the family's wealth and the heiress, Elsa, died from suicide. William J. Lemp, Jr. followed the family's tradition and shot himself. The remaining sibling, Charles, led a reclusive life after the tragedies and also shot himself.

The Lemp Mansion was later sold and became a restaurant and inn that flaunts the macabre history with murder mystery dinner theatre, Halloween parties, and dinners that leave a little chill along the spine of the guests.

"Excuse me, dear."

Olivia jumped nearly to the ceiling.

"Didn't mean to startle you," the white-haired librarian apologized. "It's just that you've been in here past your allotted time. Do you want to extend the amount of time you signed the books out for?"

She looked at her watch. It was 1:40 p.m.

"Oh my, I have to get back to work." She stacked the books quickly.

"Easy with the books please."

"Yes, yes, of course. I'm sorry. "

She scurried with the books to the front counter. The gentleman kept up with her effortlessly. "Can we just jot the names of these books down on a piece of paper really quickly?"

He reached into his pant's pocket and extracted a square piece of paper. "I thought you would ask for this." The list was neatly written in pencil. He handed it to her along with her belongings that had been sequestered during her book viewing.

"Thank you so much!"

She nearly ran from the empty library to her car and jumped in, tucking the piece of paper in her purse. After the second stoplight, she drummed her fingers on the steering wheel. Being late at the agency was not well received. And finding designer jobs in this town was not easy.

The car behind her honked as she sat longer than expected when the light turned green... Her mind had drifted.

Could the tunnels under the Lemp Mansion connect underground to the Art Museum?

TWENTY-FOUR

"It's too far Liv! Do you know how many miles that is?"

"No."

"Hold on, I'm in my car running to an offsite meeting. Let me check my GPS... Wow, the Lemp Mansion is 7.6 miles from the Museum!"

"That is far. Still, no one would expect someone to be that far from the Museum..."

"Impossible. We have to come up with a plan B."

"I can't go back to that library today. I'm already so late for work that I'll likely get the evil eye from my creative director."

"Drop by my place after work. Meanwhile, I'll be thinking about this too."

"Ok. I just got to work. Gotta fly."

Nearly tippy-toeing past her creative director's office, she thought she was in the clear.

"Olivia!" he barked.

She circled back. "Yes?"

"Where have you been? You know we're on deadline for that annual report! And it's a public company. No wiggle room on their timing."

"I had car trouble when I went out for lunch. Don't worry, the design is nearly complete. I'll have it to you by COB today."

"Our client is on the East Coast, so that's before four Olivia."

"I'll have it ready even before then."

She could have sworn she heard him growl as she turned and rushed to her desk. What an ogre.

As she worked feverishly on the design, thoughts about the tunnels kept entering her mind. At three-thirty she uploaded the design and e-mailed her boss. Five minutes later she was checking Google maps to see how far it was from the Art Museum to the St. Louis Arch. The arch located along the banks of the Mississippi in the center of the downtown. Surrounded by busy traffic and pedestrians, she could blend into the background. There would have to be tunnels in that area. And she could catch the downtown metro to the airport for a flight to Cairo. She felt her heart beating faster as she realized that the plan she and Jonathon had devised was starting to become reality.

Two hours later, she finished the revisions the client had sent her creative director and rushed to her car. Fifteen minutes later, she scrambled up the stairwell to Jonathon's condo.

The consummate host, he had stopped to get her favorite Cecil Whittaker's crispy thin crust pizza and Italian salad. The patio table was set with a festive checkered tablecloth, bright yellow plates, utensils, and a bottle of Merlot. Jonathon preferred the European style of dining alfresco whenever the humidity dropped to a level of near tolerance.

"I checked the mileage. It's closer than the Lemp Mansion."

"Not by much, Liv."

"It's 1.6 miles closer and is less likely to have blocked tunnels."

"But it's six miles. And then there's those little problems of utility lines, sewage, and some of the most dangerous gangs in this country."

"Do you really think the gangs are in the tunnels?"

"I'm sure they use the tunnels in the downtown and north city area."

"I really wouldn't want to run into them when I'm down there by myself."

"We wouldn't want to run into them in broad daylight on a busy street."

Olivia sipped her wine carefully. Her excitement from earlier today shifted to nervousness. Were they crazy to try to pull this off? Would she be able to play her role so flawlessly that no one would suspect?

She felt Jonathon's hand cover hers. "Are you sure you want to do this?"

"You're such a mind reader. I'll admit I'm a little nervous. This will be the biggest thing I've ever done in my life."

"I understand if you want to bow out. I can figure a way to do this myself. And I'd much rather you not be in danger."

"Absolutely not. I wouldn't let you attempt this without me."

"So, you're ready to become a cat burglar?"

"You've been watching too many old movies. Besides this heist will involve a dog, not a cat."

"Now, if we could just get you in a black bodysuit, that would distract the attention of any law enforcement." He winked.

"The idea is to avoid their attention."

"True. So are we going through with this Liv?"

She thought about the Museum director, who died mysteriously, and the board chair, who had just been inexplicably killed. There was no way she could live with herself if Miles was also murdered. And the fact that he was next in line was undeniable. The curse, as strange and different from modern thinking it might be, was behind all of this.

Not that she understood how the curse worked. Perhaps through metaphysical ways or through an individual. But the stolen faience, at the epicenter of it all, had to be returned.

The Museum clearly had no intentions of returning the highly prized and valuable artifact. She did feel that it should ethically be returned to its homeland since the acquisition was questionable.

It belonged in Egypt. This was undeniable.

But principles and artistic passions aside, her love for her ex-fiancé was driving her to plan the heist. They had to save Miles before it was too late.

"Liv?"

"Yes, Jonathon."

"Is it a yes?"

"Yes, we have to get the faience returned to Egypt."

By two in the morning they had talked about a list of possibilities for getting the faience out of the Museum through the underground maze of tunnels.

Having worked at the Museum for years, Jonathon knew tunnels connected with the basement of the building. Security had always been tight in the basement area, but he was a close friend with one of the guards. The guard was working on his thesis for his Master's degree in Archeology. He'd interviewed many people at the Museum regarding the Egyptian collection since his thesis was on Egyptian archeology.

"So do you really think you can trust him?"

"He's really passionate about Egyptian archeology. I'd call him a purist. As I dimly recall, his thesis had something to do with the environmental impact on artifacts when transported from their natural habitat. He wasn't very happy about our acquiring more Egyptian pieces and introducing them to our humid environment. Of course they're protected during transport and the humidity levels are monitored, but his analysis was fairly convincing about some levels of impact."

"Sounds like he might be supportive of the faience returning to Egypt. We probably shouldn't give him any details about our less than scientific method of transport."

"I'd skip that part."

"I wish we didn't have to include anyone extra in this though."

"I know. But there is really no other way to get access to all the areas without him. My access is limited like most Museum employees. The exception is the guards."

She sighed in submission. "Then we'll just have to trust him."

They munched on the remaining pizza, Jonathon offering the last slice to her. She accepted with a smile. If it wasn't for pizza, she would be ten pounds lighter. But it was the Midwest; the tolerance level for a few extra pounds was higher here compared with her rail thin friend Jill in Washington, D.C.

Between work and her upcoming new career as a "cat burglar," she wasn't going to add to her stress level by unreasonable dietary expectations. She gobbled down the last decadent slice.

"I am concerned about one area of our plan though."

Dabbing the corners of her mouth with the napkin, she asked, "What's that?"

"Getting past customs in Cairo and getting the faience into proper hands once there... You know, little details like lifetime imprisonment in a foreign prison."

"No worries, I have that all figured out. At least part of it."

"Really? Well, do share."

"There's someone I met recently who I'm sure will help us."

Jonathon leaned forward, one hand covering his mouth with trepidation and curiosity.

She sipped the remainder of her wine.

"Liv, don't be coy."

"It's just a bit of a long story."

"I have nowhere to go until 8 a.m."

"Can we go inside? The citronella candle is used up and the mosquitoes know it."

After clearing the patio table, they settled into the living room couch and she started with her introduction to Amro at the Art Museum the night the director was murdered. How the guard had helped them exit out the back and they had disappeared in her rented limo. About the connection between them. The phone calls and coffee shop meetings.

"So this guy is your boyfriend now?"

"No. But he'd like to be. "

"And you would trust him with your life in a foreign country where you have no citizenship and few rights if captured?"

"Yes."

"Liv, are you thinking this through or are you being influenced by this guy's pheromones?

"He's Egyptian. And he believes in the Egyptian curse. I'm sure he'd be considered a hero for helping with this return. Plus, he said he was connected with the Egyptian art world."

"And he just happened to be at the Art Museum the night the director was killed?"

"So was I, but I had nothing to do with the murder either."

"What's the name of this guard that helped you escape? I'm not sure what I think about him knowing a guard at the Museum. It has to be the same one that I was talking about."

"Amro's uncle has a background in Egyptian art and with the guard's thesis work there must have been a connection. He said the guard was a friend of his father's."

"Makes sense. But do you know where Amro was the night the board chair was murdered?"

"I tried calling him that night and couldn't reach him. Turns out he was in Cairo. His brother was in a bad accident…"

"Ah, the family emergency."

"Jonathon! His brother was badly hurt."

"I don't know about this guy. It all seems a little coincidental."

"I don't think so."

"You've been influenced by more than the magic of the faience, Liv."

She tapped her refilled glass of wine like an annoyed cat swishing its tail. "Do you have any better ideas for an accomplice with an Egyptian passport?"

TWENTY-FIVE

The milky gray light of dawn saturated the living room where they had spent the night debating about two accomplices that each had an opposition to – the Museum guard and Amro. But it seemed that there was no way around their critical roles. They needed the guard for security access at the Museum. And they needed Amro to safely get the faience into the proper hands once in Egypt. So they agreed to work separately with their accomplices. Jonathon would work with the guard. Olivia would work with Amro. And they would not divulge one another to their accomplice. This was one pot that did not need any extra stirring.

As dawn whispered its way into their discussion, they talked about which tunnels to use in the labyrinth. The distance between the Lemp Mansion tunnel and the Museum was daunting. The chance of running into a blocked area of the tunnels was also high since Highway 55 was between the two locations. Olivia thought the tunnels that snaked under Forest Park and to the St. Louis Arch was a strong option. The distance was 1.6 miles less. Still, it was a formidable six miles. Underground.

She presented her idea of dressing as a bag lady. The faience would be stashed in an old sack. If the police or St. Louis Arch park rangers noticed her, she would just start begging for money. She even proposed to rub some aged sausage over her body to give herself that aromatic authenticity.

But Jonathon was concerned about the distance and the time to walk that far underground. He was also emphatically worried about her running into gangs and real homeless people under the city. The faience might not ever see the light of day. And she might end the next morning floating in the Mississippi River.

Perhaps it was fatigue, but she was starting to agree with him. The thought of being underground and bumping into some of the most dangerous thugs in the nation was causing a lump to form in her throat.

The glint of the first rays of morning sun shot through the living room drapes. Jonathon sprung up from the couch and clapped his hands like a scientist who had just discovered a new gene. "I've got it!"

"Geez Jonathon, you scared me. I almost tinkled on your couch," she laughed and then was unable to stop herself from laughing uncontrollably.

"Don't get punchy on me." He shook her shoulders bringing her out of her sleep-deprived giggle.

"So tell me then what have you got? Cause what I got is to go to the potty," she giggled.

"Go. I'll make coffee. Lots of coffee."

The aroma of the coffee drenched the now sunny condo when she returned. He brought the stronger than usual coffee to her with the care of an attending nurse. After a few restorative sips, she felt her curiosity building.

"So your idea…"

He set his coffee down and positioned himself in front of her, on his knees Catholic Mass style. "This is perfect. While you were in the bathroom I checked the mileage. It's less than one mile!"

"That sounds too close. If we screw up and the alarms go off, the cops will cover Forest Park like a wet blanket."

"Forest Park yes."

"Where else would be that close? A MetroLink station? They'd be all over those too."

"No, not a MetroLink station." His eyes sparkled in the bright sun.

"Is there a street or a home that the tunnels open up to?"

"Even if there was, not a good idea."

She hugged her coffee mug to her chest. "Tell me."

He held her legs and pulled himself closer, whispering, "Washington University."

Stunned, she was frozen in his bright smile.

"Of course. Jonathon, you're brilliant!"

He laughed with delight.

Olivia jumped up nearly spilling her coffee. "I could be a student. A Master's level student of course. There won't be any shortage of students running around campus. Lots of backpacks. Too many to search. And that would be an infringement on the students rights."

"Exactly."

"But I need a reason to have slipped into the tunnels."

"Please don't say you'll be making out with Amro."

"No, that could be compromising."

"To say the least."

"Now if I was chasing something in there it would make sense."

"Chasing something?"

"Yes, like my little dog."

"You don't have a dog."

"Not yet..."

He nodded approvingly. "You're more clever than I thought, Miss Katz. This field just might suit you."

She winked at him. "It just might."

———

Walking back to her apartment, as Jonathon headed to work at the Museum, she dialed Amro. She wanted to catch him early in case he was leaving for work. And she bristled at the realization that she did not even know where he worked.

"Olivia? Where have you been? I haven't heard your voice in so long."

She couldn't help smiling. His voice was like warm honey on a hot biscuit. "Amro. Good morning."

"Good morning, Olivia. It's so nice to say that to you. Are you ok? Everything is alright, yes?"

"Yes, yes. Everything's fine. I just wanted to invite you to something tomorrow." Since she had politely rejected his advances a few days ago, she thought spending some time with him would keep their connection.

"That sounds nice. What is it?"

"I've decided to get a puppy..."

"That's so sweet. You'll be a wonderful mom to this little puppy."

She tried to wipe the sappy smile off her face. "Do you think so?"

"Absolutely. This will be one lucky little pup."

"Do you want to go?"

"I wouldn't miss it. I'll pick you up tomorrow. But I am working tomorrow to catch up on some projects that got behind when I was in Cairo to see my brother."

"Is it one of those uptight corporate environments that forces you to work through your weekend?"

"Not corporate, but uptight about projects."

"That's funny, I realize that I don't even know what field you're in."

"Information systems. Olivia, I can't wait to see you tomorrow." He clicked off blowing her a kiss.

The next morning he pulled up to her apartment building. She was waiting outside. He was wearing jeans and a pressed cotton shirt. So that confirmed that it wasn't a corporate job. Not that she really needed to know. She just wanted the comfort of knowing a little more about the guy she was going to entrust with her life soon.

She hopped into the car. He smelled freshly showered and lightly cologned.

"Where to?"

"Huh?"

"Where do you want to go look for this puppy?"

"The puppy, yes. You smell so good you had me distracted." She smiled at him coyly.

He smiled back. "It's your day Olivia. Where to?"

"So let's head to the Humane Society and see what they have. It's at 1201 Macklind Avenue."

As they drove, he reached over and held her hand. "What kind of puppy do you want?"

"Something small, less than fifteen pounds."

"Why so little? Don't you like those labs or golden retrievers that are so popular here in the U.S.?"

"Well, it's better for a small apartment. And you can take them to friends' houses easier… and they're easier to travel with. A friend of mine says you can take them inside the plane with you if they're under fifteen pounds."

"So this puppy is going to be traveling the globe?"

"I think she will travel some."

He looked at her from the corner of his eye. "Olivia, you're up to something I can tell."

"Why do you say that?" she put on her most innocent face.

He laughed. "You forget about our connection, darling."

She was a little put off by how well this guy already knew her. Still, since the topic had been started, she might as well jump in now. "I am looking at something that I may need your help with."

Again he laughed. "See, I know you Olivia. I'd love to help you with whatever you need. Tell me more."

When she played a character like the heiress at the Art Museum her finesse was impeccable. Her timing, her words, her cadence was like a well-oiled machine. As herself, sometimes her finesse was lacking. This being one of those moments, she blurted, "I'm going to steal the Egyptian faience and return it to Cairo."

Amro slammed on the brakes in the middle of Macklind Avenue. Screeching brakes behind him made her shoulders crunch preparing for an impact that didn't happen. One car swerved around them, the driver swearing as he passed.

"Did you just say you're going to return the faience to Cairo?" She looked down at her hands realizing the absurdity of her statement. "Yes."

"And how do you plan to do this?"

"I have a friend that works at the Museum who's going to help me."

Another car veered around them honking.

"You didn't tell me about this friend."

"I know. It's all very complicated."

"It must be."

She looked over and saw that he had suddenly shifted into a mood she hadn't seen in him. He was looking at her with distrust.

"Amro, don't be upset. We haven't had much time together to share everything."

"I understand. But considering that we both met at the Museum and have an agreement to not go there again, this is something that you might have told me. And how are you going to get this faience if you don't go to the Museum?"

"I'm not the one taking it from the Museum."

"You want me to steal the faience?"

"No. Not at all. Look this is complicated. Can we talk about it after we get the puppy? Because right now we're going to die of a collision before there's any opportunity for the heist."

He looked up and realized another car was screeching its brakes behind them. Stepping on the gas, he avoided the impact by inches.

They drove the rest of the way in silence.

As they walked towards the shelter, Olivia turned and took his hand. "Amro, I promise you I have the best intentions here. I know this might sound really crazy but I want to make sure that the artifact is returned to its rightful place and that these murders at the Museum stop."

He sighed. "This is an honorable thing. But you really shocked me with this idea."

"I know. Please don't be mad." She circled her arm around his back.

"It's impossible to be mad with you. But we need to talk about this very seriously Olivia."

"We will. This is not something I'm taking lightly, believe me."

A family walked through the doors with a wagging-tail golden retriever on a leash. The young boy was petting the dog and beaming at his parents.

"Let's go get your puppy Olivia."

As it turned out finding a small dog puppy or small dog adult was not so easy. The woman reviewed their options – the adult dogs included two labs, one German shepherd, a St. Bernard, the golden retriever that was no longer available, a mixed hound, and four pit bulls and the puppies were lab and Rottweiler mixes. However, there were several cats available, mainly grown, but a couple older kittens.

Olivia assured her she was definite about the small dog. It could be a puppy or adult though she conceded.

They left with a printout of rescue groups of small breeds. Olivia called the Papillon group first. She had seen these adorable dogs before when she was on Michigan Avenue in Chicago. The breed was perfect in size and had the upscale attitude that would work well for her role in the heist. She smiled as she clicked off her Blackberry. "They have an adult female in Maryland Heights!"

One hour later, Olivia was leaving the home of the foster family after providing a donation, signing all the paperwork including her work history and references, and submitting to an interview that reviewed her commitment to a long term relationship with her new family member. The adorable Papillon was licking her face as they got back in Amro's car.

"I've got competition for your affection now." He smiled petting the silky hair of the red white and sable colored dog with black markings on both her trademark butterfly like ears and at the corners of her dark eyes. "And what will be the name of this little beauty?"

She stroked the dog's sweet face. "Cleopatra."

Holding his hand to his mouth blocking his laughter, he asked, "Serious?"

"Yes. What's wrong with that? Did you see her pretty eyes?" She held the dog up for his view. "Are you making fun of her name?"

He cleared his throat. "No, of course not, darling. She does have the eyes for this name."

After stopping at the pet store and stocking up on pet food, toys, water and food bowls, and a carrier, they headed back to her apartment.

To her surprise he didn't try to invite himself in. "Thank you Olivia for a wonderful day."

"But it's only two o'clock. Don't you want to play with Cleopatra?"

"That would be enjoyable, but I promised my work that I would be back in the afternoon."

She wandered if he was put off by her idea of the heist or just playing a little bit of cat and mouse. If Amro didn't help her get through customs in Cairo, her chances of getting arrested increased significantly. Still, she didn't want to seem too needy.

"Thanks for helping me find the puppy Amro." She gave him a quick hug as she hopped out of the car clumsily holding Cleopatra and lugging the pet store bags.

Later when her Blackberry rang, she raced to answer it hoping it was Amro reassuring her that they were linked.

"Liv, it's Jonathon. I don't have much time right now, but I wanted to let you know that I've decided to go to Paris..."

"Paris? Are you crazy? We have to figure out how to get this faience back to Cairo and there's no time to spare. What if something terrible happens to Miles?"

"Calm down, please Liv. I'm not going for fun or even for business. It's just become amazingly apparent to me that we are about to embark on an international heist of property that belongs to my employer."

It was hard to argue with that.

"So, I just need to make one-hundred percent sure that this artifact was purchased improperly and that we really need to look at this as an Egyptian curse before we move forward."

"Jonathon, are you getting cold feet?"

"Not at all. I just need to make sure we're absolutely doing the right thing."

"And how will going to Paris help with this?"

"The dealer whom the Museum purchased the piece from is in Paris."

"I see."

"As luck would have it, I talked with my father this morning. He's in New York City on business and is flying back on his private jet this evening. I've booked a hellishly expensive ticket from St. Louis to New York to join him."

"I'm just worried about the timing…"

"Forty-eight hours that's all I ask. I've asked Miles to lay low for two days."

"You know he won't do it. His job is everything to him. And with all of this going on, the Museum has to be depending on him more than ever."

"You're right, I'm sorry to say. But this piece of our research cannot be overlooked."

She sighed, knowing he was right. But the queasiness in her stomach told her that the clock was ticking.

"I do have some good news for you though, Liv. My accomplice, the security guard, and I had a very pleasant conversation. He's not only willing to help us out, he lit up with excitement about the idea."

"Wonderful! That's good news."

"And did you talk with your Egyptian friend?"

"Yes and no."

"Meaning?"

"We kinda went and got the little dog today and then got distracted. He had to rush to go to work…"

"So you have your homework when I'm gone. I've been thinking about it Liv. Even though I don't feel real good about this guy, I think we need him. Getting through Egyptian customs could be tricky otherwise."

"Believe me, I've been thinking about that." She could hear Jonathon's car door buzzing in the background and the sounds of shuffling.

"I'm at the airport now. Take care of yourself when I'm gone and get his absolute confirmation that he'll help you. No maybe's."

"Got it."

"See you in two days."

The phone connection ended and with it she felt suddenly alone.

Two days wasn't long. Unless you were thinking every minute about an international heist. And how to get your new undefined relationship to help with a heist at a museum in a country where he wasn't a citizen and then to help you enter his country with a stolen artifact that was the find of not the century, but the centuries.

Would his honor bring him to help her and return the faience to its rightful place in Cairo? Of course, there was a real opportunity here for him to make millions if he snatched it from her and sold it on the black market.

Her stomach was feeling even queasier now.

The
CURSE

TWENTY-SIX

⁓

Jonathon boarded the American Airlines flight with his one bag and a worried mind that exceeded the weight of any luggage. What seemed so long ago now, his only worry had been how he was going to repair his professional relationship with Miles after their philosophical argument about the Museum's role in purchasing the faience. He was a purist and didn't believe that art should be purchased if there was doubt about its line of acquisition. But Miles, in his avant-garde and aristocrat way, dismissed this as naïve. The black market was a real temptation for everyone including legitimate and respected museums. Miles considered it an act of artistic preservation to get the artifact off the black market. Otherwise, they would likely be destroyed from neglect or disappear into hidden private collections remaining underground for generations.

There was validity in Miles' viewpoint, but the Egyptian curse brought a new level to the situation. Anthropologists had been dancing with and around the curse for centuries. But the trail of unexplained deaths was undeniable.

He couldn't let this curse from the region of the river of the Nile stretch its magical deadly spell across the world to the serpentine banks of the Mississippi and end the life of his colleague. Or, even more jarring, the harm or death of Liv.

And he knew there was no stopping her from the idea of the heist. So naïve and passionate about art, Liv was determined to take the biggest risk of her life. And he knew that she was depending on him.

His interest in protecting her - from a dangerous heist in St. Louis, the precarious return in Cairo, and the amorous pursuit of Amro - was beyond their friendship. Miles had once taken her heart; he was not about to let another steal it this time. Or put her in danger...

He had to go to Paris and check out this art dealer. Just to be certain that the deaths of his Museum's director and the board chair hadn't been from some other strange circumstances beyond the curse. The coroner's reports were unresolved. Both had died of asphyxiation likely due to a drug. Probable homicide was stamped on both reports.

Tension at the Museum had escalated. Everyone feared someone or something that had killed the top people at the institution. To his surprise, most of the employees believed it was the curse.

Each death was at the time that the faience was supposed to be unveiled. It seemed that the faience was determined not to be shown in a land that was not her own, a place where she had been brought against her will. The thought left a deep chill in the Egyptian Wing. Few wanted to enter the area any more. The Museum staff practiced the buddy system. No one was alone in any room or hallway at any time.

Liv had no idea how bad things really were. But he didn't want to worry her. She was already upset enough. At least when she wasn't talking about the new Egyptian guy.

Now that was something for him to worry about. How had this guy come around with such amazing timing when the first death happened? Could he somehow be involved? Was he a catalyst to the magic? Or something more?

He had suppressed his suspicions hoping it was a touch of fate. This new friend of Liv's could help them get the faience back to his homeland, ending this horrible curse. And then Miles and Liv would be safe.

Before leaving St. Louis, Jonathon had stopped to get a newspaper at the corner news store. Turned out that Omar was familiar with this new friend of Liv's. Knowing that Omar's brotherly protectiveness for Liv would intervene, Jonathon explained that this Egyptian had romantic interest in Olivia and it was his "brotherly" duty to check this guy out.

Omar provided him with Amro's full name, address, and employer. And Jonathon provided a generous contribution to the fund for Omar's family to come to America someday.

His father's research team would handle the rest of it.

He leaned against the curved lining of the airplane panel and looked out the window at the twinkling lights of small towns dotting the Midwest. The low growl of the plane lulled him to sleep disturbed a few hours later by the pilot's voice announcing the landing at LaGuardia Airport. An hour later he boarded his father's private jet.

"Jonathon. Good to see you!" His father patted him on the back. His crisp white shirt looked freshly pressed, as did his suit pants. Always the consummate businessman, he never showed too much affection in front of his reports. Two senior executives, who had been with his father for years, extended handshakes. A new face, a young female executive, leaned forward from her seat to greet him. She handed him a manila folder. "The research team completed the project your father requested for you."

His father's corporate team was frighteningly efficient.

He left them to their business chatter and found a seat in the back corner to review the "project."

Inside the folder were two pages of information on Amro:

Name: Amro Katar
Age: 32
Height: 6'1"
Parents: Yousef Katar (deceased) and Aziza Katar
Siblings: Four brothers
Visa: U.S. active, no marks
Employer: Gateway IT Consulting
Criminal History: None
Credit History: U.S., good

Jonathon was starting to relax. This guy seemed pretty trustworthy. He turned to the second page that offered just three more categories.

Military: Yes, Egyptian, Officer

Degree: equivalent – Bachelor's in Information Systems and Bachelor's in Anthropology

Relative of interest: Uncle, Dr. Hasaneen, Egyptian Head of Antiquities

He reread the last category four times before it sunk in. Dr. Hasaneen was Amro's uncle. "Oh my God!" he muttered. The folder slipped from his lap.

The attendant hurried back to his seat. "Sir, are you ok? Is there anything I can get you?"

Jonathon shook his head.

His father walked back to his seat. "Everything ok son?"

"Yes, yes. Just a little surprise." His button-down shirt father would never understand that he was in the middle of an international heist to return an Egyptian faience to Cairo. And now he had just found out that his partner in crime had been at the scene of the first murder with the nephew of the world-renowned Egyptian head of antiquities who was demanding that the artifact be returned to his country.

What a bloody mess.

"We're going to lower the lights and catch some sleep before we land in Paris in the morning at six. My day is jam-packed, but feel free to meet me later tomorrow around five at the usual café for a glass of wine."

"Sure Dad. That would be nice."

A quick pat on the shoulder and he was gone. The consummate on-time and well-prepared executive, even in his sleep schedule.

The lights lowered as Jonathon's mind entered the maze of the puzzle he needed to figure out to keep himself and Liv from going to prison.

Or the morgue.

TWENTY-SEVEN

t six the cabin lights activated. After a few foggy seconds, Jonathon gathered his wits enough to realize he was in his father's private jet. Stuffing the file on Amro into his one piece of luggage, he tucked his wrinkled shirt into his pants and ran his fingers through his hair attempting to look presentable.

As they departed, his father patted him on the shoulder, "See you this evening at the corner café." He had on another perfectly pressed shirt underneath the elegant Parisian suit; his hair combed back European style. Always dressed immaculately for the event and the location.

Jonathon looked like he had slept in his clothes. "Mind if I stop at the apartment for a quick shower Dad?"

"Not at all, we'll call ahead to make sure Henry is available to let you in." He turned to ensure that the assistant had heard him. She was already on her Blackberry calling the butler.

———

"Monsieur Bonné such a pleasure it is to see you." Henry opened the apartment door. "Will you be staying long, sir?"

"Just overnight. Then we're headed back to the States."

"Very good, sir. The bathroom is ready for you. And we'll have breakfast on the patio as you like."

Jonathon wondered why Henry always spoke in English to him, but spoke in French to his father. Perhaps he was being gracious not to expect Jonathon's French to be perfect after living so long in St. Louis.

The bathroom claw foot tub was already full of warm water, and fresh white cotton towels lay on the chair beside the tub. Henry had been in his father's service for as long as he could remember. He knew Jonathon's every preference - the olive oil soap, the lavender shampoo, and just a few bubbles. It would be so easy just to bathe, wander down to breakfast, and then sink into the plush bed. But there was no time.

After breakfast, he would head over to meet his contact at The Louvre and find out more about the art dealer. The pastries and coffee on the patio were beyond any experience he could replicate back home. It was interesting that he thought of St. Louis as home now. For so many years, he thought of Paris, where he was born and raised until his parents divorced, as his real home. But time and distance had changed him. He truly felt American with Paris as his second home.

During breakfast, Henry had pressed his clothes from his suitcase. His other clothes were gone, no doubt being properly laundered. He sighed pleasantly. This much attention was just too easy to re-acclimate to.

Maybe Liv would consent to a little trip to Paris in the future. It would be fun to see her spoiled and to enjoy the city together.

But for now it was time for research. Parisian-style of course.

The car dropped him at the side entrance of The Musée du Louvre.

The front entrance was already littered with a meandering line of tourists who would wait for hours before entering the doors of the most significant art museum in the world.

His friend, Alexandre, was graciously nearby, conversing with a colleague near the side door. "Ah, Jonathon, please come join us!"

Quick introductions and the colleague politely left them. It was hard to be irritated with such hospitality, but still Jonathon wished someone would speak to him in French. Even when he spoke in French, they politely responded in English. Very well, English it would be then.

"So we go to my office and I can show you a couple things about your project," Alexandre invited.

They headed along the elegant hallways with soaring ceilings to the administrative section of the museum. Even after so many visits to The Louvre, Jonathon was awed by the ambiance of such powerful works of art displayed in striking architecture that drenched the senses in periods of the past.

In Alexandre's office, they sat at a tiny round table. His desk was stacked with columns of books and folders in no specific order. "Now where is that printout…ah, still on the printer of course," he laughed. "Let's see, this art dealer you asked about. We have some information on him too. He's still living here in Paris. I have an address here for you. We have heard a few things about him though, Jonathon…"

"Oh, and what have you heard?"

"Well, it's not so good."

"Please, I need to know as much as you can share."

"Well, we have heard that he is not someone to trust. That his papers are not complete in most cases. But worse yet, in some cases they are contrived."

"This is what I was worried about."

"I'm so sorry Jonathon. We heard that your Museum has purchased an exquisite Egyptian piece from him."

"Do you think the artifact is real or that it was not properly documented?"

"Oh, it is very, very real. This is most certain."

"How do you know for sure?"

"Well, Dr. Hasaneen knows this. And he wouldn't be spending his valuable time traveling to St. Louis to try to get it back of course."

"Of course."

"And one other little thing…"

"Yes?"

"The dealer offered it to us at one point."

"Alexandre! You're sure it is the same piece?"

"Absolutely Jonathon. But we could not take it because the papers were not legitimate. And believe me when I tell you that this was one of the hardest pieces for us to turn down. It is the find of the century, my friend."

A quick knock at the door ended their conversation as a young intern provided tiny cups of cappuccino in white china before darting out and closing the door snuggly.

"And now Jonathon you must have quite a dilemma."

"So you've heard about the two deaths at our Museum?"

"Yes, yes. The whole world has heard this."

He sipped the cappuccino delicately.

"Tell me, Alexandre, do you believe in this Egyptian curse?"

Alexandre looked at his Italian shoes and removed one tiny speck of paper dust from his creased trousers, then shrugged, "Yes, of course, I have to say that I do. There's just too much of a pattern that has not been seen other places. But tell me why you ask. Do you have doubts about this?"

"No, I believe this too…"

"Ah, maybe you have a little doubt. This is natural. And you are a logical thinker raised by a father who would not sponsor such thought, yes?"

"True."

Alexandre leaned in closer, his eyes squinted thoughtfully, "My friend, the most powerful things in life are not logical. Religion, love, war… none of this is logical. But from the beginning of time, people have died for these things and risked anything."

Jonathon felt a rush of urgency surge through his body. Slowly a line of goose bumps started along his arms and made a trail to the back of his neck. Time was running out.

"Would it be too rude to ask for that art dealer's address? I'm only in Paris until tomorrow."

Alexandre handed him the paper with the address. "Not rude at all. It seems there might be something you need to handle quickly."

They walked to the side door where his father's limo was waiting. The driver raised his brow slightly when he looked at the address. It was not a part of Paris where limos usually ventured.

As it turned out, for good reason.

Jonathon checked the address from Alexandre's print out. It was correct. But the limo had pulled up in front of an abandoned warehouse. He called his father's assistant who checked their significant resources to only come up with the same address for Kafele Bedon, a gentleman of Lebanese and French background. Who apparently was shy about providing a real address. Unless he had an unusual apartment tucked away in the warehouse.

"Please wait for me here, I'm going to check to see if anyone lives in this dilapidated place," he instructed the driver.

"Yes, sir," the driver replied nervously.

Jonathon pushed the creaky two-story door open slightly. He slipped through the narrow crevasse.

The cavernous warehouse was empty. Daylight spilled from the damaged roof to the dingy concrete floors littered with trash and discarded bottles of cheap wine.

Determined not to have come all this way for a dead end in an empty building, Jonathon walked past the debris to the back of the building toward a walled off section with a door. The doorknob, cold in his hand, twisted begrudgingly. Inside the room was an office with an old desk but a new computer, phone, and a comfortable looking couch.

"Bonjour?"

A door slammed from deeper in the office and a skinny, scraggly bearded man in his fifties entered the room cautiously.

"Oh hello!" Jonathon accidently spoke in English.

"Ne parle pas anglais…"

"Parle francais."

The man looked at him skeptically. Jonathon's accent was weak clearly. He wrote down the name of the art dealer with a question mark, sure that his pronunciation would not be accepted.

"Ne Kafele Beton."

He asked where Kafele might be. But the man just looked at him. Finally, he wrote it down on paper in French. But again the man just looked at him. Perhaps the universal language would work better. He pulled out some cash from his wallet.

The man looked at the amount and leaned closer to see what remained in his wallet. Jonathon gave him the rest. The man nodded and wrote down an address.

As he left, Jonathon looked over his shoulder a few times. A shadow passed by his foot before he made it to the door. Rats were his least favorite creatures. He picked up the pace to a near run and thankfully slipped through the massive warehouse doors and into the afternoon sunlight.

The driver looked more pleased by the next address. Back to civilization. They drove a few miles from the warehouse and pulled up to a tiny Lebanese restaurant. Only eight empty tables were inside.

Jonathon greeted the waitress and asked for Kafele Beton. Her lips pursed into a circle as she fled to the back room. He waited. Minutes passed before a heavy set Lebanese man came out to see him. Distrust etched into his wrinkled forehead.

Two minutes later, Jonathon left the restaurant with yet another address. Since he had already given away all of his cash, he devised a story about a contact telling him to find Kafele to purchase art for his private collection in America.

The next address mustered an approving nod from the limo driver. Twenty minutes later they pulled up to an elegant townhouse. Jonathon's knock brought a butler to the door who assured him that no one named Kafele was there, but that the lady of the house would be willing to talk with him about his art interest for his American collection.

Jonathon waited in the contemporary parlor that resembled a French design magazine. The butler provided him cappuccino as he continued to wait. Forty minutes later, the lady of the house entered the room. He had expected a more mature woman given the level of comfort and services. To his surprise, a model thin twenty-something woman flowed into the room. Her long black hair and the striking features reflected Arabic roots. Not that he wanted to sleep with her, but he was thrown off center by her sensual aura.

"Good afternoon, Mr. Smith," she chanted.

Jonathon had decided it was best to give the butler an alias.

Completely comfortable, she joined him in a cup of cappuccino and started into small talk about the Parisian weather. Her English, although not perfect, was good. An hour later, they started to talk business.

"Mr. Smith, you've been so charming to talk to. But I'm afraid I have nothing for you to take back to America on such short notice."

"I completely understand. Is there any way I could talk with Kafele. My buyer would like to ensure that I can reach him later for our acquisition."

"Yes of course. But I'm sorry to say that I've lost contact also with Kafele."

"You have?"

She pouted. "He was suppose to visit me a few weeks ago, but no."

"How strange."

"Yes, very. It has never been so long that I hear from him."

"Do you have another address for him?"

"No, just his cell number. And now that no longer works."

She looked genuinely upset.

"Is there anything I can do?"

"Well, perhaps. But no, it's too dangerous." She flipped her long hair over her shoulder and shook her head dramatically.

"Please, I want to help," Jonathon played along.

"Well, I know that sometimes he would go underground to connect with his art world contact…"

"Underground?"

"Yes. The tunnels under Paris."

Jonathon's heart froze. Was this a set up?

She saw his hesitation. "Oh, see, it's too crazy. Never mind, Monsieur. I'm sure he'll call sometime…"

"Are there many tunnels under the city?"

"Oh, yes, they're famous!" She laughed. "Dangerously famous."

"Would you know which one he would have gone to?"

"I do. One time when we were coming back late from a club, I made him show me. I wanted to go into the tunnel. But he not let me do this. Too dangerous for a woman."

Jonathon twinged at the thought of the plan to have Liv go into the tunnels in St. Louis.

"Mademoiselle, please let me help with this." He took her hand and looked into her eyes with all the Good Samaritan acting that he could exude.

"You sure?" Her perfectly plucked eyebrows peaked.

"Yes."

"Ok, your man can drive us?"

"Of course."

The sunlight intertwined with afternoon shadows as they left the townhouse. Ten minutes from her place she insisted that they stop.

"This is it!" She pointed to an alley. "You walk down there, open the last door at the building end on the left and go down stairs. Kafele not take me in, but he say there is door inside that swings open. This is his tunnel."

Jonathon was feeling uncomfortable. He needed time to think. The driver was having a hard time not responding to the danger his employer's son was getting himself into. But the driver was too professional to do so, and Jonathon was too pressed for time to bother with thinking.

"I'll be right back then."

She grabbed his arm. "Monsieur no! You not do this in daytime." She laughed at his silliness. "No one can see you going into this place. Very secret. Do later."

Now he was feeling even more uncomfortable.

"Sir, it's after four o'clock. I believe your next appointment will be waiting."

Jonathon didn't want to be late for his meeting with his father at the café. Being late simply was not an option with him.

He wrote down the address of the building next to the alley as the limo headed back to the townhouse to drop off this strange girl whose name he didn't even know. Chatting on the way back, he tried several times to get her name, but she was skilled at aversion and slipped out of the limo never disclosing it.

On the way to the café, Jonathon's mind was racing. Should he dare to go into the tunnel by himself? What could he possibly discover there? A derelict or two… some macabre individuals that liked the alternative life… criminals that used the tunnels to run their business… high end swindlers that made a killing from stealing and illegally selling artwork like this Kafele Beton… probably a rat or two.

His thoughts turned to the mesmerizing girl that seemed so genuine in her loss of Kafele. Who was she really? Could she be a rat herself? Maybe she wanted him to disappear. She may not like strangers calling on her. Or maybe she was simply an opportunist. Accustomed to her beauty and sensuality getting her anything she wanted. And for now she wanted him to find her Kafele.

"Sir, we've arrived at the café."

His father had already arrived and was seated at his reserved table, pouring over paperwork and sipping cappuccino. The waiter delivered a platter seconds after he was seated.

Normally, Jonathon would have enjoyed the warm bread, the cheese platter, the wonderful wine, the delicious cappuccino, perhaps a crème brulee and the rare opportunity of his father's attention. But he was too distracted. So when his father announced that he needed to leave for his business dinner, he was a bit relieved. He wanted to take care of this task of searching the tunnel before he lost his nerve.

"Please stay and enjoy the café, son. I've signed for the bill. But I will need the car for the evening. In case you didn't bring euros..." his father slipped the money in his hand. "For cabs. Enjoy your night in Paris, son."

Jonathon slipped the euros in his pocket. It felt like entirely too much money for just cabs. He could never fault his father's generosity with money. If he could only be that generous with his time.

After a second glass of wine, it was time to gather his nerves and take care of the task. Using the resolve he saw in his father's tenacious business deals, he braced himself to leave the cozy catered ambience for a dark rat-infested tunnel.

"Sir, you're leaving so soon? Another glass of wine perhaps?"

"You don't know how much I'd like to say yes to that."

The waiter smiled. "So, yes?"

"I'm afraid no. But there is something you could do for me."

"Of course, Sir, anything for you." Jonathon knew that meant anything for the son of one of their best customers.

"I need one of those little flashlights you use for the patrons who can't see in the dim light."

"Yes, yes. We have plenty, of course." Reaching into his pocket he gave him the flashlight.

"Merci."

"Of course. Have a wonderful evening."

Unfortunately, a cab was waiting right outside the front door. The one time he was hoping for a cab to not be available so he would have a good excuse to not go to the tunnel. The cabbie jumped out and opened the door.

Minutes passed entirely too fast before the efficient cabbie zigged his way through the Parisian traffic and arrived at the address Jonathon had been at only a few hours ago. But now the alley was masked in darkness. The doorway to the tunnel was hidden in the inky abyss between the buildings.

The cabbie left seconds after he shut the car door. Alone in this quieter part of the city, he realized that he had left no trail should anything happen. He called Liv knowing that, without a calling card, it would cost a fortune. But considering what he had spent on the flight from St. Louis to New York, who was counting.

"Liv?"

"Jonathon? Are you ok?"

"I'm fine. Look, I need to keep this short."

"Ok, sure. What's up?"

"I need to tell you my whereabouts in case there's any trouble."

"Dammit Jonathon that sounds awful!"

"Don't panic. This is just a precaution. Write down this address and don't share it with anyone unless I don't return to St. Louis."

She took down the address and then confronted him, "Jonathon! What are you doing?"

"I'm about to go underground into a smelly, rat-infested Parisian tunnel. You do realize how much I care for you Liv?"

"Of course Jonathon. You're like the brother I never had."

He shook his head thinking that Liv was naïve about even more than the danger she was in. "I have to go now before this phone call costs me a fortune."

"Wait. Hold on. Why are you going into the tunnel?"

"It's the last place the art dealer is presumed to have been."

"Jonathon, I don't think this is a good idea... Let's talk about..."

"Liv, before I go, have you talked with Amro about helping us in Cairo?"

"Well, hold on we need to talk about your situation first."

"Liv?"

"I'm having trouble reaching him."

"Listen Liv. I may not trust this guy, but we're going to need his help. And soon."

"I know, I know. There's a restaurant that I know he likes. My friend Lisa is getting a sitter and we're going over there tonight."

"Good. The connection is fading... Gotta go."

"Be careful..."

"Love ya, Liv," he clicked off before she could talk him out of it.

Taking a deep breath, he walked into the dark alley. His small flashlight provided a luminating arrow toward the doorway at the end of the building. It seemed that all sounds of humanity had vanished. He wasn't sure if it was because of the insulation of the surrounding empty buildings or because his heart was pumping so much blood he could hear nothing else. A drop of sweat made its descent down the muscular curve of his back as he pulled the door open. Garbage-laden stairs dipped into deeper darkness decorated by the staccato clop of his shoes as he forced himself to take yet another step leading to the tunnel. As he turned left from the bottom landing, the aroma medley of urine, mold, and spilled wine assaulted his nostrils.

He flashed his light around the entrance, one hand still on the stair railing in preparation for a bolt back up the stairs. The brick curved ceiling, darkened by a moldy patina, receded into a charcoal passage. In the depths of the passage a small light came closer.

Instinctively he took a step backward. But he had come to find Kafele Beton and this could be him. Still, it was not in his makeup to want to meet someone for the first time in a lonely dark tunnel. He hesitated. And it was only his love for Liv that kept him rooted to the landing rather than racing up the stairs, flying out the door, and running down the street to jump into the nearest taxi to get far away from this dank, dangerous tube.

Taking the situation in hand, he decided a greeting might be better than to surprise this stranger. "Bonjour?"

"Yeah, sure Bonjour to you too…" The man with the flashlight continued to come closer. A man who was clearly not French.

"Hello?"

"Ok, hello, to you too…" the hyena-pitched laughter ricocheted against the tunnel walls.

It was getting harder to not bolt up the stairs.

"Who are you?" Jonathon inquired.

"I'm the boogey man." The stranger's laughter cascaded into a coughing spell.

Jonathon took another step backward. "Are you Kafele?"

"Fuck no." The stranger appeared into the dim light of his tiny restaurant flashlight. He was a slim and tall American. At first, he felt relieved. Until he realized that this American was no comrade. Hair thick with debris and shiny with oil, he smiled into space, eyes clouded by his drug-induced state. A heroine addict was not whom Jonathon wanted to meet in this empty tunnel that likely did not have cell phone access.

The weight of the euros in his pocket reminded him of his father's resupply of cash. He would try to act casual, like he hung out in underground tunnels often. "Hey man, sorry to bother you. I'm just looking for this guy Kafele. You know him?"

"Yeah, he's back there." The addict pointed to the deeper recesses of the tunnel.

"Thanks man! Here's a little something for the favor." He handed him a generous amount of euros.

The man's eyes slightly focused on the money and a slippery smile crossed his face. "Nice. Time to get me another hit." He passed Jonathon and headed up the stairs to make his street connection.

The dark recesses where the addict had pointed did not look inviting. Every instinct in his body was telling him to leave, and fast. But he pushed on, forcing himself to take one step after another into the claustrophobic depth. He had not gone far when he tripped over something. Shining his light to the right, he gasped.

A man's body was sprawled on the moldy tunnel floor. Face down, his dark hair well manicured. His clothes expensive and fashionable. Body rigid.

Could this be Kafele?

Jonathon shined the light in an arc around the tunnel, wondering who might still be around. Could this have been the addict's work?

There appeared to be no trauma, no blood. Just a collapsed dead body. Just like the director and the board chair at the St. Louis Museum.

He was having trouble breathing. Panic took over. The tunnel walls felt narrower. The darkness thicker.

His light caught the raised form of a wallet in the back pocket of the body. There was only one way to find out for sure if this was Kafele. Gathering his wits enough to think through the possibility of a police investigation, Jonathon grabbed the handkerchief that his father's butler Henry had so carefully put into his pocket this morning. How very long ago that seemed now.

With his forefinger and thumb he wiggled the wallet out of the man's pocket, his prints guarded by the shield of the perfectly creased fine cotton handkerchief. He slipped it open to read the identification… the license had a picture of a man who looked Lebanese and part French. He drew his penlight closer to the plastic covered card and leaned forward to read the name. Kafele Beton.

He could no longer control his reflexes. Like a sprinter jumping forward at the sound of a gunshot, he ran, his heart rushing, his legs pumping adrenaline-filled muscle to move faster, plowing through the darkness to the landing, scissoring up the stairs two at a time, and exploding into the night air. He finally stopped running six blocks later when traffic and couples walking along the sidewalk surrounded him.

His lungs aching, he dropped onto a bench.

The
RETURN

TWENTY-EIGHT

"So how long have you guys been dating?" Lisa quizzed her on the way to the restaurant. Once again, Olivia had stretched her story a bit. They really were not dating. Flirting was more precise.

"Not long. But I just have this sneaky suspicion that he's double-timing me."

"Why are men such jerks? I swear in the past year, I've had three girlfriends going through the same thing. If I ever thought my hubbie was trying that game, I'd …"

"Lisa, you missed the street. Bar Italia is one block back."

"Sorry. Can you tell I'm an old married lady now that never gets out? I used to know the Central West End like the back of my hand."

They circled around the streets hunting for a parking space.

Olivia was starting to feel that she was outgrowing this area. She observed the same groups, the samereactions, and the same predictable behaviors. Young girls in skimpy clothes talking too loudly to get as much male attention as possible and the college guys pushing one another around and talking equally as loud to show off their masculinity. The young professionals were less demonstrative, scattered amongst the crowd in small groups or on dates. A few middle-aged couples dined al fresco and people watched. And tonight there was Lisa and herself on their stalking adventure.

She was getting the jittery feeling that caused her to flick her foot rhythmically like a cat's tail. If Amro had gone AWOL she could be in a tight spot. Getting through Egyptian customs with a stolen Egyptian artifact would be tricky. TSA might not recognize the faience at the Lambert-St. Louis International Airport, but Cairo International Airport would be a different story. She imagined explaining to the Cairo police that she was returning the artifact to Dr. Hasaneen.

Visions of life in a Cairo jail played and replayed.

"Hey let's get a table over there by the tree with the cute little lights. I just love eating outside like this. It's so European you know." Lisa skipped over to the table like it was her first night out in years.

Olivia surveyed the restaurant guests, looking for Amro. No sign of him. But it was still early. During dinner, she was too distracted to keep up with her friend's barrage of stories about the kids, her husband, her house…

And then she saw him. He walked straight towards her with a cute little blonde. Before he saw her, she grabbed the dessert menu and put it in front of her face.

"Oh, you want some dessert Olivia?"

"Shhh…"

Olivia cocked her head towards Amro as they passed the table. Her friend grimaced when she saw the girl.

It had to be the longest thirty minutes in a restaurant she'd ever experienced. The waiter took Lisa's dessert order and left with a puzzled look when Olivia refused to return her menu to him. She continued to sneak glances at Amro and the blonde. When they started smooching, she had all she could stand.

Olivia walked across the restaurant, stood beside their table, and waited for the kiss to end. His shocked look was somewhat satisfying.

"Amro, we need to talk."

"Olivia, what are you doing here?"

"Let's cut the small talk. We need to talk now."

"This is really, um, strange…"

To her surprise, the girl saved the moment. "You know, I had planned on catching up with my friends over at the club." She jumped up, grabbed her purse, and jaunted away from the restaurant.

Amro nodded his head. "Well, it looks like this seat is available. Please, sit."

"Just a minute, let me give my friend some money to pay for our dinner." She walked back to the table hoping the stall would give her time to calm down. She had to think beyond her emotions at this point. His playing while she was desperate to reach him meant nothing to him. Focus, she told herself.

She dropped off the money and gave a quick explanation to Lisa whose eyes were wide with the live drama. A few minutes later, Lisa paid the waiter and waved a quick goodbye to Amro's table where Olivia had returned and sat silently.

"Look, Olivia, I'm sorry about that girl. She's an old friend that was in town and it was only a dinner, believe me."

"We have more important things to talk about right now."

"We do?"

"Yes. I need for you to arrange my visa and to help me get through customs in Cairo," she whispered.

"Excuse me?"

"You remember what we talked about in the car when we were picking up Cleopatra? Or is my new dog also out of sight, out of mind?"

He skimmed right over the jab. "You mean the..." he looked around conscience of the close tables with curious diners.

"Yes, that item that needs returned."

"You're really serious about this?"

"More serious than I've ever been."

He nodded. "Then I will do this for you."

"For me?"

"Yes, and because I think this is the right thing to do."

She leaned in and looked unwavering into his eyes, "I have to have your absolute promise that you'll be there for this. It would be very risky otherwise."

He laughed. "It's risky anyhow, darling." His hands curled around hers. They felt warm, protective. "I'm in, Olivia."

"One hundred percent?"

His dark eyes penetrated hers, "One hundred and ten."

She nodded and grabbed her purse.

"Where are you going? Don't you want a drink?"

"Not tonight."

He nodded sheepishly. "I understand."

"Amro, I need for you to be completely available by phone tomorrow so we can settle on the plans, ok?"

"Absolutely."

Walking home all she could think about was how right Jonathon was about this guy. What were the chances that Amro would really help them?

But he was Egyptian. And for him, it had to really be more about getting the faience back to his country.

After taking Cleopatra for a short walk, she slipped into bed. Growing up, bedtime meant a prayer before sleeping. Comforted by the childhood practice, she prayed Jonathon was safe.

Tomorrow he would be back in St. Louis.

And it would be time to begin their plan.

TWENTY-NINE

———

The Blackberry woke her at six, thirty minutes before her alarm was scheduled to go off. Cleopatra yipped at the intrusion. She really disliked the sound of the Blackberry. Olivia agreed. It was like having an ankle bracelet to her employer.

"Hello?" she mumbled.

"Liv, it's Jonathon!" He sounded shockingly alert for such an unreasonable hour of the morning.

"Thank God you're alive! Where are you?"

"I'm on my father's jet. We just landed in New York and I'm about to catch my flight to St. Louis."

"That's the best news I've heard in a long time Jonathon! When will you be in St. Louis?"

"In a few hours."

"Wish it was sooner. I'll be at work already."

"The good news is that I survived the nasty Parisian tunnel…"

Olivia sat up in bed, the adrenalin waking her like a cold shower.

"What happened?"

Cleopatra started yipping in earnest at the Blackberry.

"What's that noise?"

"It's Cleopatra. She hates my Blackberry."

"Smart puppy. Liv, I can't go into a lot of detail at the moment, but let's just say it was not a pleasant experience."

"When exactly will you be back in St. Louis?"

"Before noon. Let's meet for lunch and I'll fill you in. Bar Italia?"

"That's the last place I want to meet."

"Why? You love that place. Oh no, what happened?"

"I'll fill you in over lunch. J Buck's in Clayton at one?"

"See you there."

Olivia clicked off and grabbed her sweat pants and sneakers to take her impatient Cleopatra for a quick morning walk. Realizing she had not checked the news in more than 24 hours, she stopped at the newsstand to pick up the morning *St. Louis Sun Journal.*

"She's so sweet, Olivia," Omar beamed at the little Papillon. "What a lucky little dog this is. Maybe she is being rewarded for her hardship at the animal shelter."

"Omar, she was there for one day." Olivia laughed. "I think you're right though, she's a lucky girl. Maybe she will bring good luck to me also?"

He nodded and with complete resolve said, "Yes. I'm sure of this."

"Good! Well, since she doesn't fetch, I'll have to pick up this paper myself and buy it."

Omar laughed. "She doesn't look like the kind of dog that would fetch."

Cleopatra looked up at him and Olivia would swear the little dog smiled at him.

Laughing, Olivia waived and headed back to the apartment. When she opened the folded paper, the smile dropped from her face. Front page, top story, the headline read:

Museum Closes Egyptian Exhibit as Investigation Escalates

After two murders at the St. Louis Museum of the top executives, board chair Dr. Jacobs and museum director, Dr. Schneider, the museum board voted unanimously to close the Egyptian Exhibit until the police investigation has been resolved. The exhibit has been void of visitors since the incidents. According to a museum source, guests have been frightened of the Egyptian curse which Dr. Hasaneen, head of Egyptian antiquities declared in a recent press conference to have been connected with the deaths. The renowned archeologist has visited St. Louis in a vigilant pursuit of the museum's return of the faience to Cairo.

The Art Museum is under a cloud of suspicion for their connection with the art dealer, Kafele Beton. Notable art museums around the world have refused to work with Beton after several art pieces resulted in unsubstantiated paperwork and a murky procurement path. The Louvre, The British Museum, and the Metropolitan Museum of Art confirmed that he is on their list of no procurements.

Since the two murders at the St. Louis Museum, the French-Lebanese art dealer, who lives in Paris, has been missing.

Olivia tossed the paper on the floor, shirking from the reality of the curse. All she wanted to do was pack her bags, grab the faience, and get on the next plane to Cairo. To make sure that this beautiful and dangerous artifact was returned to its homeland. To know that Miles was not going to be the next to die from the curse.

But this had to be done right. She wanted to walk away from this a free woman.

She sighed and headed to the shower. This was going to be another brutally long day at the agency.

Olivia had no more walked in the door of the agency when her creative director accosted her. "Olivia, where the hell is the redesign for the Dairy Association's annual report?"

"I'm sorry, I know it was due Friday. I'll have it finished in two hours, I promise."

"You've got one hour. Is there something you don't understand about this business and deadlines? Do you know the shit I got from the client this morning? I don't understand what's going on with you. This nonsense has been going on now for two weeks."

"I've had some things on my mind. Doesn't the years I've worked here and met every single deadline count for something?" she snapped. Her director's glare made her regret the outburst.

He leaned toward her close enough that she could smell the coffee on his breath. "I have a stack of resumes in my desk of graphic designers who would love to work here, miss. You know, designers that understand deadlines."

Olivia stared at him in shock. Two bad weeks and one missed deadline and he was threatening her job. She rushed down the hallway to her workstation. The possibility of losing her job was not what she needed on her mind right now. And how was he going to react when she took a couple impromptu days off work to return the faience to Egypt.

Should she call in sick? Claim a family emergency?

She wasn't sure if either situation would work with him given his current state of mind. What an ogre.

One hour later, she uploaded the new design on the FTP site and e-mailed him a profuse apology. Better to play it safe with him. Finding another graphic design job in this area was not easy.

Her friend Jill in Washington D.C. had the opposite situation – designers whimsically came and went when they had their feelings hurt or felt like their project loads were unreasonable. Maybe she should consider her friend's offer to connect with her association's creative director.

Could she really leave St. Louis after living here her entire life except for the few years in New York City? Then again, she wondered if she could really stay if she did lose her job? And there would soon be the matter of having committed an international crime?

Letting out a huge sigh, she delved into her folder of pending projects keeping pre-occupied throughout the morning.

Lunchtime. She grabbed her purse and snuck out the back hallway to meet Jonathon. J Buck's was just a few blocks away. She discretely left her car and walked, avoiding her boss's side of the building. Just in case he would be looking out the window and be ready for another confrontation when she returned.

At the restaurant, the waitress whisked her to the back. Jonathon had thoughtfully selected a private booth. He always managed to get the table of his choice. Good training from his father, no doubt.

He looked up from the menu, eyes gray and scooped with puffy bags. His hair had been finger-combed. The blue striped shirt was rumbled. "Jonathon, you look awful."

"Thanks. It matches how I feel."

Olivia shrunk into the booth and grabbed his hand. "What happened in Paris?"

He shook his head as the waitress returned and cheerfully took their salad orders.

"Jonathon, tell me what happened…"

Running his hands through his hair, he took a deep breath, looked around the restaurant to make sure no one was nearby, and in one breath poured, "I found the art dealer who has been missing, the one that sold the faience to our Museum. In the tunnel."

Olivia leaned in closer. "What did he say?"

"Nothing. Absolutely nothing."

"Well I'm not surprised. You know he's not going to want to look guilty in this case…"

"No, that's not it."

"No?"

"He was face down dead Liv."

Two plates of salad, efficiently delivered by the waitress, separated them. "Will there be anything else?" she asked cheerfully.

Jonathon nodded. Olivia stared at him, unable to speak. The waitress pivoted and addressed her next table.

Minutes passed as she watched him stuff salad into his mouth. Her perfectly arranged salad on the chilled white plate sat before her untouched.

"I've already researched the flights to Cairo." He slipped her a handwritten note. "Here's the airline and flight that departs Wednesday night. I'll cover the expenses. But you'll need to book the flight in your name. And arrange with Amro for his flight to be at the same time. If you get investigated, you'll say that you left together for Cairo for a romantic trip. Of course, you won't mention this trip to anyone. Not your boss, not your girlfriends, not even your mother. "

He stuffed more salad in his mouth, sipped his wine, and continued in his monotone. "The Museum is having a benefit on Wednesday. I'll be there. My contact at the Museum will arrange to transport the faience to you through the tunnel. You'll meet him close to the underground Museum entrance in the tunnel. We can't afford for him to be out of sight too long. Bring Cleopatra in her carrier. The faience will be her doggy bowl. But absolutely no water or food in the bowl! You'll have to feed her by hand once you're in the plane. Tell Amro to pick you up on Forsyth Boulevard and drive you to the airport." Jonathon's fiercely blue eyes honed in, "Will he be there for you Liv?"

She pursed her lips.

"What does that mean?"

"He's been distracted with a blonde. They were having drinks and smooches at Bar Italia."

"Nice. That's just great."

"Not to worry. He's on board with this, Jonathon."

"Is he still hoping to win your heart?"

She laughed, "It's not about me. He's doing this for his country, his pride."

"Yes, and perhaps his uncle."

"His uncle?"

He sipped some more wine, crossing his legs smugly. "My father's highly qualified research team did a background check for me. Turns out he's pretty clean. One interesting detail though is this uncle of his."

"What could be so interesting about his uncle?" Olivia nervously stabbed at her salad.

"His uncle is Dr. Hasaneen."

Entirely too loud, she blurted, "Oh my god."

He nodded, "Precisely."

Wrapping her arms around herself in a protective embrace, she ignored the waitress who had returned to handle the situation. "Is everything ok, ma'am?"

"We're fine," Jonathon assured. He covered her hand with his. "We're going to be just fine."

The waitress left.

"There's still time to get out of this Liv. I can handle returning the faience myself. It would really be preferable. The stakes have become way too high at this point. And I don't want anything to happen to you."

"Are you crazy? You would be an easy suspect. I'm in the background. There's less of a chance of me getting caught."

"In St. Louis, yes. But I'm not so sure about Cairo."

"Amro will take care of that."

He grimaced. "Are you sure?"

"Absolutely."

Her Blackberry vibrated. She smacked her forehead. "It's my boss looking for me. He's threatening to fire me if I don't get my act together at work."

"I'm so sorry Liv."

"Gotta run. I'll sneak in the back and pretend I was in the bathroom."

"Don't forget to order your tickets and talk to Amro this afternoon."

"The tickets are for this Wednesday?"

"Yes."

"Jonathon, that's in two days!"

"We can't wait any longer. I don't want Miles to be the next one on that cold marble Museum floor."

The image ran a cold shiver down her spine. Losing her job would be worth it to make sure they did not lose Miles.

Jonathon grabbed her arm before she darted off. "Are you sure about this?"

And at that moment she knew that she had never been more resolved of anything in her life. Returning the faience would end the curse and be a crossroads for her. She knew that after this, she would never be the same again.

She imagined holding the faience, racing through the tunnel, and delivering it to its rightful home.

For some reason, when the first story about the faience broke she had picked up the *St. Louis Sun Journal* that fateful morning and read about the faience. For some reason, she had become fascinated and lured herself into attending the benefit the night the Museum director was murdered. For some reason, she had met Amro and he had helped her escape that night.

"It's my destiny, Jonathon. I must do this." The words sounded strange, ringing with melodrama. But she knew in her heart it was true.

"You're an amazing girl." He smiled. "Meet me tonight at my place?"

She nodded and ran down the scorching sidewalk to the agency.

THIRTY

"You miss a deadline and then you run off for an hour lunch?" the creative director roared.

"It was already planned. I'll stay late and catch up on my other projects."

"We have designers working sixty hour weeks and not taking lunch anytime during the week. You know, the designers that are turning out solid work and not missing deadlines. Apparently, you thought I was playing this morning when I said there are other designers that would jump at your job."

"No, really. It's just like I said there are some personal things going on…"

"Forget the sad stories. I've heard them all. Look Olivia, our agency is fighting for these accounts against a line of other agencies. I have to think of the agency first. This simply isn't working out. I'm going to have to let you go."

"You can't be serious. I've been here five years and always had good reviews."

"Well the market is getting tighter and there's no room for designers that are burned out…"

"I'm not burned out!" Olivia yelled. "Can't you just give me a week off and I promise to come back with my problem resolved?"

He paused and then shook his head. "Can't take that risk right now. Sorry about that. Drop off your pending folder on my desk and gather your personal items."

Olivia stood there as if someone had just dumped a bucket of ice water on her.

"Hey Olivia, you turn into a pillar of salt or something." Sharon chided as she walked past in the ever-narrowing hallway.

"I just got fired."

"What? You shittin' me?"

"No."

"That son-of-a-bitch. You've been here five years. And you're one of our best designers. Don't worry, I've got you covered. Just have anyone call me for a reference. I am the office manager after all. I'll just say our creative director is unavailable or left or something." Sharon patted her on the back. "Now don't you worry, you'll find a new job in no time."

"You know there aren't that many designer jobs in St. Louis."

"Well, you could freelance…"

"That's not very dependable."

"Well, you'll figure it out. Let me grab a box for you, honey. At least you don't have to put up with that tyrant any more."

The Starbucks by her place felt different on a weekday afternoon. A few freelancers were scattered about with their laptops and cell phones and a casual business meeting with two customers was taking place in the corner.

Departing the agency was a haze. Sharon had helped her pack up her stuff. She'd switched over her personal numbers from her Blackberry to her personal cell phone. And then she had dropped off her laptop, pending files, and Blackberry to her boss.

Sipping a cappuccino, Olivia started thinking through her options. Next week, she would call her friend Jill in D.C. If she had to work in D.C. for a while, that's what she had to do. Maybe a shorter workweek would allow her the time and energy to create her art again. It had been a long time since she had been in a studio. The cold clay in her hands and the whirring drum of the wheel would be good.

For now, she conveniently had more time on her hand to walk through her plan for Wednesday. After she met with Jonathon tonight, she'd have all day tomorrow to get ready and to take Cleopatra for a covert walk in the tunnel.

The next couple of hours she called or texted everyone in her address book to make sure they did not use her Blackberry number. Even though the Blackberry probably wouldn't work. Olivia had managed to "accidentally" drop the phone in the toilet before she returned it.

Before heading to Jonathon's she made the flight arrangements to Cairo for herself and Amro. The cost was insane. She felt bad using Jonathon's money for this. Still, she had no budget to sponsor the trip.

The odd sound of her cell phone caught her attention. "Hello?"

"Olivia! Are you ok? I got your text. What happened at your work?" She soaked in Amro's voice like a warm bath.

"I got fired. After five years, I missed one deadline and the jerk sent me home."

"That's so crazy. Are you alright?"

"Just a bit traumatized."

"Do you want me to come over tonight?"

She paused. And heard herself say yes. She knew she would have to be careful to not let him take advantage of her vulnerability.

"See you at nine then," he smooched.

Olivia felt like a schmuck. But soon they would have less need for one another. The faience would be returned. And she might be living in another city.

———

"Jonathon you didn't need to fix salmon and wild rice. My favorite."

She eyed the lemon-topped salmon feeling hungry for the first time that day.

He kissed her cheek as he scooped the fish onto the white plates and circled the towel around the edge for a perfect presentation. "You deserve it Liv. I can't believe that ogre just let you go for no reason. And I feel completely responsible for distracting you with this debacle going on at the Museum."

"It's absolutely not your fault. Remember, I'm the one that went to the fundraiser the night the director died?"

"Still, I could have taken more time off work and handled some of that library research…"

She shook her head. "We could play this game forever. Let's just enjoy this wonderful dinner and go over our plan…"

Jonathon would be at the Museum event and would act as the decoy. He would make sure that Brian, the guard, was there and ready to move the faience to the tunnel entrance. With it being late at night and everyone at the benefit, the basement would be empty. Brian knew how to work the security cameras so that there would be no surveillance of him in the basement. He had the keys and would ensure that the alarms would not be set. After he handed the faience off to Olivia, he would nonchalantly return to the main level, and switch the cameras and alarms back on.

"It all sounds too easy." Olivia tucked her leg underneath her and stared out the window as if the twilight sky would divulge the flaws in the plan.

"The hard part will be yours Liv. You'll have a tunnel to meander through, a little dog to keep quiet, two airports to pass through security, and then a city in another country where you've never been before and don't even speak the language."

Suddenly getting fired seemed minor.

THIRTY-ONE

Just before nine Olivia dashed out of the apartment like Cinderella rushing to her pumpkin-turning chariot. She claimed that her dog would be desperate to be let out by now, but really the desperate need was her own. Amro was on his way.

Racing up the stairs to her apartment, she grabbed Cleopatra's leash and scooped the silky yapping bundle up. How was she ever going to get through the tunnel discretely with no time to retrain her canine accomplice?

The dew on the grass was already accumulating in the humid early night as her dog sniffed every blade before selecting her spot. Waiting impatiently, Olivia was completely surprised by the warm arm that circled her waist and pulled her backwards against a tall Egyptian body.

His hot kiss on the side of her neck sent chills to her toes. She leaned into him for a moment before forcing herself to pull away.

"Amro, let's not get distracted. We have business to talk about you know."

"I'm fine with mixing business with pleasure, my darling." He leaned toward her again. But she firmly held her hand against his chest.

His pride prevented him from yet another attempt. "Very well. Business it is." He smiled at her confidently. "For tonight anyhow."

For the next few hours they talked through the plan in the privacy of her apartment. And she felt more confident that together they would make this heist happen. That he would be there for her. A warm hug goodnight made her feel even better as he slipped out the door.

Olivia slept like a baby.

Until she woke with a gasp as the first hint of dawn whispered through the curtains. When she called Amro, he immediately answered.

"What's wrong Olivia?"

"A dream…"

"Dream? What about?" he muttered.

"Miles is in serious danger…" she shivered under the warm covers.

"It's a dream Olivia. He'll be fine. We're returning the faience very soon and this will make things fine. Believe me."

She sat up inconsolable. "You don't understand. This dream has meaning. My Cherokee grandmother always said to listen to the dream. They are the spirit world talking to us…"

He was awake now. "What happened in the dream?"

"Miles was walking out of the Museum. It was late. He was by himself. The dark oak trees surrounding the Museum seemed denser, more sinister. As he walked toward his car a mist descended on him…"

"That doesn't sound good."

"No. It felt like I was losing him."

"Tomorrow is just one day away, Olivia."

"Let's hope it's not one day too late."

THIRTY-TWO

~~~~~~~~~~~

Minutes after talking to Amro, her cell phone rang.

"Olivia, it's Miles. What happened to your Blackberry? Someone at your work was very cryptic about the phone being reassigned..."

"The agency fired me."

"Sweet pea, you have to be kidding me? You've done a brilliant job there for what five years or more now?"

"I know. My work this past two weeks has been less than desired and I missed one deadline. So the ogre of a creative director fired me. All he cares about is accumulating more awards to decorate the website with and to drop into our pitches."

"Unbelievable. What's happening Olivia? This isn't like you. I've been so distracted with everything at the Museum, it looks like I've been a terrible friend and not kept up with you."

She so wanted to tell him what had been happening. But he would never agree to the heist, especially in order to save his own skin. Miles, although not the best in personal relationships, was an unflappable gentleman. In a shipwreck he would help everyone into the lifeboats refusing to take the last one so someone else would go.

"Olivia, I can break away for lunch today if you want to talk."

She nearly agreed, but realized that his comforting way and those familiar warm blue eyes risked divulging her angst over the beautiful faience and the Egyptian curse that had him in peril.

"Let's go next week. Right now, I have, uhm some things to do…"

"I understand. You need some time alone to get over this dreadful situation."

"Right."

"Now don't worry, sweet pea. I can send you some freelance work from the Museum to tide you over until you find another design job."

"Thanks Miles! I'll call you next week then."

Olivia clicked off her cell with a sigh of relief. It was going to be difficult to not tell him about the heist. After some time, it would be easier to not tell. Moving to D.C. would make it even easier.

Today her reconnaissance on the Washington University campus was the focus. Her game plan was simple: disguised as a student, if caught she would say she had gotten lost. Easy during the day.

Tomorrow night's traverse would be the challenge, especially with a dog and a stolen Egyptian faience worth millions.

The historical map that she and Jonathon had dissected showed the tunnel linking with the underground passage near the center of the Washington University campus. She remembered the maze of passages from her student days at the University. Some of the more daring students walked through the underground catacomb to avoid the frigid winter days.

She had tried once herself.

The passage, apparently used by maintenance, contained the mechanical infrastructure of the buildings. The concrete floor and dimly lit passage at first seemed fairly benign. Walking down the tunnel, lonely footsteps accompanied by a dripping sound and the slight hum of equipment changed that feeling. The emptiness of the tunnel and the unknown pathway made it instantly claustrophobic. She had been simultaneously afraid of being alone in the desolate underground while disconcerted about who would be around the blind corners.

And without the comfort of cell phone service in the cobweb-laced belly of the campus underground.

Olivia had diverted her plan that snowy January day when she was headed to her art composition class. Twirling around and bursting out of the passageway into the cold air she had sworn to never try that again.

She hadn't told Jonathon about her student experience. Nor had she mentioned that she was claustrophobic. Not a serious case, but elevators with too many people and an MRI experience made her short of breath and ready to flee.

Now she had to face the tunnels again.

Nothing to fear but fear itself, right? So a little claustrophobia, a sweet little dog whose verbalizing could ruin her, spiders, a possible run in with a home-less person or worse yet a gang member, or most frightening of all – the police. Of course, there was the added worry about Amro showing up. Would he keep his promise?

She had not told Jonathon about her concerns about Amro. The news that his uncle was Dr. Hasaneen was disturbing. And how did this guy just happen to be at a reception at the art museum the night the first victim was murdered? How did he really know the guard? The same guard that Jonathon had recruited to help with the heist. Why had Amro been so hard to reach when the Museum board chair was murdered? A sudden family emergency he had said. Interesting timing.

Maybe seeing him with the blonde at Bar Italia had escalated her suspicions. He acted interested in her romantically while dating another girl. Would his ethics be compromised in other ways?

She had a nagging feeling about him.

———

Olivia parked her aging Nissan along Forsyth Boulevard and dropped some coins in the meter. Each coin clicked like the tick-tock of an antique clock ready to chime.

Her student attire – backpack, jeans, and t-shirt – blended into the campus background. She ventured unnoticed to the building she vividly remembered exiting that snowy January day. Ironically, it was January Hall, one of the older campus buildings that housed University College, the evening school of Washington University's Arts and Sciences majors. She had taken some evening courses in the building and remembered fondly the adjunct faculty that mesmerized her with real life case studies. Those courses were some of the best of her college portfolio.

The East side of the rectangular building aligned with Brookings Quad. In the grassy square students played Frisbee and soaked up sun and conversation with friends. A stream of professor and student traffic crossed the brick path intersection through the stone arches of Brooking's Hall that overlooked Forest Park.

Olivia had fond memories of this historical university. It was as rich in the arts as it was in world-renowned medicine and science.

She darted inside the lower level side of January Hall and scooted nonchalantly past the classroom in session along her right side. The discreet narrow door leading to the tunnel blended into the white walls.

The door whined open ejecting a musty odor. The mold spores in St. Louis were prolific and in this underground passage resplendent. Could she really feel her eyes getting puffy already?

She took a deep breath and stepped into the tunnel.

A few minutes later her eyes adjusted from the bright sunlight to the dim lighting. The tunnel stretched into unknown depths decorated by pipes along the ceiling. She needed to get her bearings. Otherwise, it could be a really long afternoon wandering around lost in this claustrophobic maze.

She pulled the roll of white tape out of her backpack. Marking her way would help her remember her pathway for tomorrow. She turned right and marked her turn with the first white taped x at knee length. This tunnel had to lead her under the quad toward Forest Park.

Now that she was in the tunnel, the distance of one mile seemed significant. Jonathon had been right about avoiding the Lemp Mansion underground route that would have been more than seven miles, one way.

She sneezed. And then sneezed again. Pulling tissues from her backpack she sighed and made a mental note to take extra allergy medicine tomorrow.

Time to cover some distance. She picked up her pace and walked deeper into the tunnel resolved to wrap up this reconnaissance quickly. The walls of the tunnel seemed to be getting narrower and narrower from the descending trajectory and her ascending claustrophobia. Breathe, she told herself. Just breathe.

Deeper and deeper she continued on a straight line. The single light bulbs had now disappeared as she left the campus grounds above. The concrete floor replaced by cobblestones crusty with dirt and black mold. Her flashlight beamed ahead to a T. She walked quickly trying not to think about the increasing cobwebs and dank smell.

Catching her breath again she wondered if it was from the air quality or from her claustrophobia?

She remembered reading about the limited time Egyptian explorers could spend in some of the deeper narrower catacombs that lacked breathable air.

The worry about confronting spiders, homeless, gangs, or the police could all be small matters compared with the lack of oxygen and cell phone service for an emergency call.

Olivia stopped. Halfway point. Decision time. If she passed out from lack of oxygen, the only two people, Jonathon and Amro, who knew she was in the tunnels, would not find her in time.

Shaking off her worry, she marked her left turn and picked up her pace. There was no time for a second attempt at this reconnaissance. She had to make sure the tunnel linked up with the Museum sub-basement door where the guard would be waiting tomorrow night.

The resonating sound of footsteps in the tunnel far behind her stopped her short. She flicked off her light and hunkered down. Was there any way out of the tunnel except the way she had entered?

Jonathon had pointed out this specific tunnel from the guard's research at the Museum. But the only other exit she remembered was at the end point of the Museum underground. And she had discretely not brought the hand drawn map the guard provided.

The rustle of the steps sounded closer. A flashlight wavered in its owner hand. Feeling like a captured fox in a trap, thoughts raced through her mind – run past him, knock him down, run towards the Museum in the thin air and knock on the door. None of it made any sense. Who was this person racing towards her in this desolate cavern?

To her dismay, she sneezed.

The running footsteps stopped. "Olivia?"

"Amro?" she asked shakily.

He ran towards her and pulled her up from her crouch. "Are you ok? I've been calling your cell phone constantly."

"It doesn't work down here. How did you know how to find me? I mean in this specific tunnel?"

"I'm friend's with the guard, Olivia. Remember from the night we met at the Museum fundraiser?"

"Of course. But why are you looking for me? We're suppose to meet up tomorrow night to go to Cairo..." she was starting to feel dizzy from the poor air and the adrenaline rush.

"The guard says you shouldn't go too deep into the tunnel without some backup oxygen. He called me this morning. Then I couldn't find you... So I picked up this little portable and ran down here."

Reaching for his backpack, he pulled out a portable oxygen device used by patients with chronic respiratory problems. She had seen her friend's grandmother use one.

"Where did you get this?"

"Medical store. Don't worry, I paid cash. Just put this thing on." He wrapped the tubes around her and turned on the battery-operated device.

She breathed in the sumptuous oxygen. Was she really that short on good air? Her lungs craved more and more of the oxygen. She sucked it in like a diver who had gone to deep and returned to the surface gasping.

Amro kissed her and turned to leave. "I have to get back to work before I'm noticed missing. Call me as soon as you get out of the tunnel, understand?"

She nodded as he turned and escaped the musty tunnel.

A few minutes later, she realized she was still standing in the same spot, stunned. This web between the guard, Amro, his uncle Dr. Hasaneen, and Jonathon was becoming tighter. Was it a dream catcher she wondered or a trap?

She was in way too deep to escape the web now. The only way was to move forward. So she headed deeper into the tunnel toward the Museum door. The passage was clear, but thick spider webs laced her hair and backpack.

The tunnel curved to the right as she tried to remember detail from the hand-drawn map. Ahead, within the beams of her flashlight, she saw the door. A heavy metal door that looked impenetrable. The Museum had taken no chances of anyone sneaking in this way.

They hadn't figured on a guard opening it from the inside within the secure subterranean level where the faience awaited her.

She turned back, her reconnaissance completed.

The path was clear.

The guard was ready.

Amro was ready.

Her heart raced as she ran the distance back to the tunnel campus entrance. A much shorter distance it seemed when returning.

But she knew the return of the faience would be either the longest or the shortest two days of her life.

THIRTY-THREE

ednesday morning she woke with a start. Dreams toyed with her throughout the night... she had forgotten her passport... forgotten her e-ticket with her confirmation number... forgotten the portable oxygen device.

She splashed water on her face staring at her puffy eyes, the result of troubled sleep and the mold from her traverse in the tunnel. Dabbing gel under her eyes, she darted back into the bedroom and began to pack with the precision of a parachute instructor. Triple checking everything before loading it into her on board size suitcase, she started packing the backpack she would use in the tunnel.

Amro was picking up her suitcase this afternoon in advance of the heist. Roaming about the campus this evening with a suitcase would draw attention. And it would be clumsy to manage and ensure the safety of the faience.

After he brought her the oxygen yesterday, her trust in him had increased somewhat. Still, she packed her passport, license, credit cards, and airline e-ticket in her backpack. A little caution never hurt anyone.

To calm herself, she headed out for a morning run and cappuccino. Cleopatra joined her. It seemed too far for such a little dog, but she had relentless energy. And she would be cooped up for a long flight tonight. Fortunately, she was carry-on size also, small enough to fit under the airplane seat.

Jogging through Forest Park, Olivia went through every step of her plan.

She was nervous as a first-marriage bride. The jog was a mild sedative for her nerves. Cleopatra was completely exhausted she was happy to see. She needed her to be calm tonight when they were in the tunnel. No yipping.

She stopped to pick up a magazine at the news store.

"Olivia! Hello, miss. How good to see you and your beautiful dog."

Omar could bring sunshine into a room on the gloomiest of rainy St. Louis days.

"Hello, Omar. How are you doing?"

"So good, miss. So good. I think my wife will be coming to America soon."

"Really? Omar that's amazing." He had been talking about saving for his wife to come for as long as Olivia had lived in her apartment, more than five years.

Omar's joy was overwhelming him. His smile was beautiful. "God is good."

"When will she be coming do you think?"

"We think in one month."

"I'm so happy for you, Omar!"

He smiled gently at her, "Now something good is on the horizon for you too, miss," he tapped his heart, "I feel this. A good thing I feel."

His words were exactly what she needed to calm her nerves. She smiled from the heart as she paid for her magazine.

Cleopatra yipped as they left the store.

Olivia sighed. This yipping thing would be her undoing she was sure. What kind of international heist could take place with a barking dog?

If there was only time for training classes. Or an intervention by the Dog Whisperer.

An hour later, after a cappuccino and magazine browse, they were rushing home. Amro would be there soon. Showers were in order for both her and Cleopatra.

In the afternoon, Amro picked up the suitcase and chatted for a while. He could tell she was preoccupied.

She hugged him goodbye and promised to call him as soon as she had the faience and left the tunnel.

The afternoon sprawled before her laboriously ticking away like an old grandfather clock… She called friends. She watched interior design shows. She read one of her favorite Anne Tyler novels. There was no distraction that could make the time move faster.

Early evening tippy-toed in at Chariots-of-Fire slow motion rate.

When her cell phone rang, she knew that time had finally shifted. It was Jonathon confirming with her. "Liv, I'm headed to the Museum. I've confirmed with the guard. He's ready." He paused and the tone that only an old friend has came through, "There's still time to change your mind, honey. Are you ready?"

"Absolutely ready. Everything is packed and prepared."

"You're amazing, Liv."

"Perhaps amazingly crazy. Can I tell you something Jonathon?"

"Sure."

"I've never been more excited in my life."

"Ah, the adrenalin has kicked in already," he laughed. "But be careful. Remember what is at risk here. I want to see my beautiful friend again, not read about you being locked up in an Egyptian prison."

"Amro will take care of me."

"Oh, I'm not positive about that, honey. Don't let him swoon you."

"It's going to turn out fine, I feel it."

"Good. But please, please be cautious. I'm at the Museum. Liv, it's time for the return to begin."

"I'm on my way. Love ya, Jonathon."

"Love ya, too, you crazy girl."

She clicked off her phone, grabbed her backpack, and zipped Cleopatra into her new soft-sided traveling carrier.

The heist had begun.

THIRTY-FOUR

⁓

Inside the Museum, Jonathon attempted to keep up with the fundraiser small talk. Chatter ricocheted throughout the columned grand entrance, diffused by the splashing of the center fountain. The sumptuous smell of elegant appetizers was no decoy for his undeniable worry about his closest friend Liv and what she was about to attempt.

She was grossly unequipped for such an adventure. There was not a criminal bone in her body. How had he allowed her to get into such a dilemma?

His guilt was starting to overwhelm him. He had to admit that his love of the faience had blurred his thinking. Olivia had yet to see it. But even in the dim tunnel, she would be mesmerized.

When the faience had first been delivered, Miles had shown it to him. The beautiful turquoise bowl had a charisma, a power unlike any art piece he had ever experienced. Whispers from centuries past seemed to have penetrated its ceramic body as the lotus design etched inside the bowl drew him closer until he was unable to resist touching the faience with his bare hand. Miles had pulled his hand back, an understanding smile crossing his face.

He had teased Liv about being under the spell of the faience. But was he also? Is that why he wasn't stopping his friend from risking her freedom? Is that why they both wanted to make sure Miles' life was spared but also deeply wanted this undeniable artifact returned to her homeland?

Jonathon also worried about Amro. Beyond seeming like a player, he had been oddly unavailable when the Museum board chair died. Then there was that little situation of his uncle, Dr. Hasaneen, the man who was vehemently trying to get the faience returned to Egypt.

If Amro was greedy or wanted to erase his trail, the news would be bad for Liv.

Jonathon had a toxic mix of excitement that the faience would be returned, but dread that his friend may pay the price for the heist. He set his untouched plate of hors d'oeuvres on the platter of the circulating waiter.

THIRTY-FIVE

⁓

The tunnel smelled even worse at night. Humid night air filled the entrance of the tunnel as Olivia, weighted down by her backpack and portable oxygen tank, tried to manage a confused Cleopatra in her carrier. Fortunately, the confusion was acting as a barking preventative.

She flashed her light around the bottom of the tunnel checking for her tape markings from yesterday. The bright white of the tape connected with her light. She decided to remove them as she left. No need to leave her fingerprints for law enforcement should they check the tunnel after the faience was discovered missing.

As the descending tunnel transitioned from the concrete floors to cobblestone, Olivia extracted the oxygen from her backpack.

Her heart beating faster. Closer now. In just minutes she would have the faience in her hands.

She stopped, covering her mouth studiously, as the weight of the situation enveloped her. How did an aspiring artist with a perfectly clean criminal history and good credit score get herself involved in an international heist? Could she blame this on the spell of the faience? Or perhaps the magic of Amro?

In her heart she knew that both of these played a role. But it was more than that. She may never be involved with Miles again, but he was the love of her life and she was determined to save him from the Egyptian curse.

And yet there was even more to it. The need to achieve something far greater than a recently fired graphic designer in a struggling advertising agency would ever think possible. A way to forever be a part of restoring art history by returning this faience to its origins as the artist would have wanted. As King Tutankhamen and his mother would have desired.

Burial grounds were sacred in her Cherokee heritage. So much Native American history had been disturbed and taken for greedy purposes. She understood the outrage of Dr. Hasaneen, of Amro, of the museum guard, of Jonathon.

It was time for her to return the faience.

Olivia picked up her backpack and unzipped Cleopatra's carrier. She would need to alternate giving herself and the dog oxygen as they entered the deepest and most remote part of the tunnel.

The rest of the tunnel seemed a blur as Olivia could only think that each step she walked was a step closer to the faience. Mold, spiders, and the darkness were only in her peripheral vision. A few times she slowed to clumsily give herself and the dog some oxygen. The oddness of it all had left the dog speechless. Not a single bark.

As they turned left at the T toward the final bend of the tunnel, Olivia realized she was clipping along at a near jog. She slowed, knowing the guard had timed her arrival.

A trickle of sweat trailed down her back. The backpack was getting heavy. The tunnel was getting deeper.

The beam of her flashlight illuminated the Museum's underground steal door. Catching her breath, she walked up to the door and waited. Exactly on the hour as they had determined, the door slowly creaked open with a reluctant wrenching sound of an entrance that had been sealed for decades.

Would the cello like screech resonate throughout the tunnel or be heard in the Museum?

To her horror, Cleopatra bolted inside the Museum. Olivia made a dive to catch her tail but the silky hair slipped through her hand.

Through the crevice of the partially opened door, Olivia could see a strong hand clasp the back of the dog's neck and pick her up like a wet rag. The dog was handed to her from the now visible arm as the door opened. The guard had managed to sweep up the dog with one hand, maintain the security of the faience in the firm grasp of his other hand, and prop open the door with his foot. They stared at one another in silence.

He nodded toward the dog carrier.

She snatched Cleopatra and tucked the dog away.

In a whisper so low she had to lean in closer to the door, the guard instructed, "Keep the faience wrapped until it goes through customs. Only have it unwrapped when the dog is not in the carrier. No food or water can be in the carrier. Absolutely nothing in the faience. Keep her wrapped when on the plane. No exceptions."

She nodded.

He looked her over as if he needed reassurance that she could be trusted with one of the most valuable Egyptian artifacts to be found in centuries.

Slowly and deliberately he handed it across the Museum door's threshold into the tunnel and her waiting hands. It was wrapped thoroughly and she could not see even a hint of it in the shadow of the light extending from the Museum's basement. But as the wrapped package transferred to her hands, the energy from the faience radiated throughout her, warming her body and filling her with an unexplainable excitement.

Her eyes connected with the dark and determined eyes of the guard. He nodded.

Olivia awkwardly responded, "Thank you for your help."

He smiled sadly as if he had just sent his best friend on a plane to never be seen again. For a final time, he looked at the faience veiled by layers of protective packaging. "Take her home."

The door closed.

Olivia delicately placed the faience inside the carrier and scooped up the dog in her arm. Her neck muscles tightened as the weight of the care of this historical artifact hit her.

The return through the tunnel was a blur. She was filled with the wonder of this amazing piece of art that she now had in her possession. On the black market, the faience would be worth millions. And she was carrying it through a tunnel in a dog carrier.

She had expected to be struck by the beauty of the piece when she saw it. The power of its energy was difficult to understand. How could this art be so powerful, so magical?

Before she realized it, they were back to the campus entrance. Olivia set Cleopatra down to make sure that the carrier was fully zipped. Smelling the fresh air, she bulleted toward the door yipping with wild abandon just as it swung open.

The campus cop scanned her, taking in her backpack, dog carrier, and shocked look. "What are you doing in here, miss?"

Think fast, she told herself. Her mind was still clouded by the faience's energy. How was she going to convince this cop that she had gotten lost when she looked like she was about to take a trip somewhere?

All the restraint of not barking in the tunnel had filled the little dog with an uncontrollable burst of yips. She jumped around in circles just outside the open door which Olivia would have given anything to get through if the cop wasn't blocking it. "Can I get my dog, please?" Olivia smiled sweetly. "I just don't want her to get away from me again. She's in training."

The cop stood aside as Olivia darted through the door gingerly keeping the carrier perfectly balanced as she swept up Cleopatra. "Bad doggy. You know you're not to run away. Remember your training, sweetie." She smiled again at the cop. "I'm so sorry. She's had me running all of this campus. I had her in this carrier because I'm meeting a friend here to help him study. And, as you can see, I can't trust her to stay with me when she's walking. Last week, she completely slipped out of her leash and took off, nearly running into the traffic," Olivia touched her chest with feigned alarm, noticing that the cop also became distracted by her well-endowed bosom.

"So my vet said to get a carrier for her until she gets through her training class," she leaned in closer to the cop and whispered, "I have to tell you though she's not doing very well with her classes."

The six-foot well built man now seemed as confused as Cleopatra had been in the tunnel. "Oh, I'm sure she'll do fine." His eyes still had not left their exploration of her chest.

"Well, let's hope so. I'm really embarrassed by her running me around like this. She had to do her business so I just let her out of her carrier for a minute and then someone opened that door into that nasty passageway and she ran right in it. Did you know there are spiders in there?"

"Yes, miss. I'm sure there are. Do you need some help getting her in the carrier?"

Her blood ran cold. This silly damsel in doggy-owner distress act would fall flat if he saw the neatly wrapped package.

"Well, that's so sweet of you," she smiled ever so sweetly again. "But she has some business to do first."

"Right. Well try to keep her on a leash or in the carrier, miss. Dogs aren't allowed to run free on the campus. That passageway is just for maintenance also."

"Sure thing. I'm determined to keep her corralled. And you won't see me going into that spidery passageway again." She shivered for effect.

He chuckled. "Have a good night."

"You too. Bye now."

As he walked up the sidewalk and turned past the building, Olivia allowed a sigh of relief. Close call.

Now she was late. Amro would be waiting for her. She hoped.

She headed past one of the modern campus buildings, McDonnell Hall, toward Forsyth Boulevard. The street was filled with parked cars as she searched for him, trying not to panic. Half a block down, headlights flickered. He was here.

She nearly ran toward the car as he pulled out from the parking spot and met her halfway. He leaned across the passenger seat and opened the door from inside the car. Handing him Cleopatra, she opened the back door and daintily tucked the carrier behind the seat on the floorboard. In the front seat, she tossed her backpack on the floor and jumped in.

He could see the alarm and excitement in her eyes. "Did you get it?"

She nodded.

"What took so long?"

"I got stopped by campus police when I came out of the tunnel."

"What happened?"

A car behind them honked.

"Let's get to the airport, Amro. It's ok, I just made up a silly story about Cleopatra running into the tunnel and that she was in training class and not doing very well and that I was trying to meet a friend to study and she needed to do her business and then ran off…"

"And he bought this?"

"I'm not sure if he was really even listening. He kept staring at my chest."

Amro laughed. "I have to say this quality of yours is really distracting."

Olivia stared ahead down the long narrow street. The close call had left her with an adrenaline down.

And she still had two airport customs to get through.

THIRTY-SIX

~~~~~~~

The gravel lot of long-term parking struck a reality chord. She realized that they needed to review their game plan. "Amro, I'm going to continue with the dumb-blonde act since it worked on the campus. So don't be surprised if I act strange."

"What a shame. A beautiful brunette like you playing the dumb blonde. This is so not like you."

She managed to bite her tongue and not respond that he didn't seem to mind blondes like the one she had seen him kissing at Bar Italia. It was not time to be petty. "And we'll need to act cozy like we're lovers going on a romantic trip together?"

"Act like. You mean we are not?" He gave her that sexy smile.

She wasn't sure if it was the distractions of the night or if she had already started separating from him, but it wasn't working on her this time.

"Amro, we have to be focused."

"Wow, such a director you are now."

She rubbed her forehead. "No, I'm not being bossy. I just want us to get the faience returned and not go to jail."

He rubbed her leg gently. "Me too, Olivia."

The commuter bus pulled up alongside their car.

Perfectly synced, as only two connected people can be, they silently grabbed their belongings. Amro slung her backpack over his shoulder and nestled the dog under his other arm. Olivia gently retracted the carrier from the backseat and carried it on her lap during the bumpy ride to the terminal.

They had one hour before the plane departed. Plenty of time.

Following the guard's instructions, Olivia headed to the Starbucks bathroom just outside of the security gates. Amro waited for her along the cold wall. Her nerves were on end from the constant announcements on the overhead speaker... passengers rushing to get to their planes... security's watchful eyes and cameras. She needed to calm down. They would smell the fear on her.

The Starbucks one-person bathroom with a lock provided her with privacy she needed. She delicately unwrapped the faience. It had been masterfully packaged – secure but relatively easy to extract from the bubble wrap and blanket of pristine cloth. As the cloth fell from the bowl, Olivia heard herself gasp.

She had seen a photo of the faience in Jonathon's apartment after the *St. Louis Sun Journal* story first broke about the museum piece.

Nothing could compare to the real thing.

As if she had slipped back in time to centuries ago, she could feel the gritty sand that filled the air as the artisan poured his soul into the bowl commissioned for King Tut's mother.

Even in the metallic light of the airport bathroom, she saw the amazing color of the faience, the lotus enticing her to come closer as she lost all sense of fear, of time, of reality. Olivia drifted into its magical beauty … absorbing a sense of connectedness with pure art and its overwhelming power. Power to deliver a message to the soul. Power to fill others with greed.

That power was now in her hands as she held the faience, the cloth respectfully protecting it from the oils of her hands as she drew it closer and stared into the depths of the lotus.

A firm knock at the door startled her.

"Someone's in here," she answered.

She tucked the faience into the carrier.

From the other side of the door, she heard, "It's Amro. We're going to miss our plane if you stay in there much longer."

Trying to sound casual, she responded, "Sure. I'll be right there." She wondered how long had she been in the bathroom staring at the faience.

He was waiting, impatiently. "Olivia, do you know how long you've been in there? We could miss our plane. Let's go."

They rushed toward the security gates.

Greeted by a line that was crawling along at a painfully slow pace, Amro and Olivia sighed simultaneously. The waiting was starting to play tricks on Olivia's mind. She was sure that security was watching her. More security had arrived and was milling about behind the gates. Had they been called to handle them when they came through? Had the faience been reported missing? Was the airport already on watch for passengers who looked suspicious? Perhaps someone carrying the faience in a dog carrier and traveling with an Egyptian man?

"Olivia, look at me," Amro directed.

She looked at him, her forehead lined with worry.

"You have to get that glaze out of your eyes or we're never going to get through customs."

"But they've got more security all of a sudden. What's that all about?" she whispered.

He smiled casually at her and chuckled. "It's simply time for them to change shift. They do that you know." Circling her waist with his free arm, he pulled her close, kissed her gently, and soaked her up with his eyes. "Nothing to worry about, Olivia. So get that glaze out of your eyes before we go through customs, ok?"

Her self-control with this man had just evaporated with a single kiss. He had completely distracted her from all of her endless worry.

The line moved forward. Her heart jumped as she realized it was their turn.

They set the backpack and then the dog carrier with the faience gently into the grey container and on the conveyor. It trailed along behind another plastic container as they walked through the security portal and showed their ID to the agent who waived them through. As they passed the agent Olivia felt the weight of worry on her shoulders drop away.

The sharp staccato of the alarm pierced through her like a dagger. The agent turned to survey them as he held out a hand to the next passenger to halt.

Amro slipped the backpack over his shoulder as they waited for the dog carrier and unwrapped faience now under the scrutiny of the TSA.

For once, Cleopatra's bark was perfectly timed.

"Shhh baby, they'll have your carrier through in a moment." Turning to smile at the agent inspecting the bowl, she continued, "She thinks you're trying to take her favorite bowl."

The trio of agents looked up from their inspection. "This is an unusual bowl," the agent whose gloved hands had withdrawn the bowl observed.

"Oh thank you. My friend made it for me. She's a ceramics artist. Just finished her MFA at Washington University. It's supposed to look Egyptian to go with my Cleopatra's namesake. Not that I would say anything to my friend, but I don't think it really looks Egyptian. Seems more Greek to me..." she babbled.

"I think it looks Egyptian," the agent interjected.

"You do?"

The other guards nodded in agreement with the agent.

"Well, I guess so."

Amro played along and nodded, agreeing with the agents.

"Oh my gosh, you do to?"

He nodded again.

"Well, he should know he's Egyptian. We're on our way now to our first trip together to Cairo." She snuggled up against Amro.

"That's nice." The agent surmised as he returned the faience to the carrier bored with the interaction.

The agent at the gate slid his eyes up and down Olivia and smiled. "Lucky guy."

She smiled coyly as the carrier slowly rolled toward them. Picking it up before the next plastic tub bumped it, she forced herself to casually slip her shoes back on and head toward the plane.

Minutes later, she had slipped into the next bathroom, rewrapped the faience, and carefully stuffed her little confused dog into the carrier's corner as they entered the plane.

Amro tucked the carrier under the seat as he snuck Cleopatra beneath his left arm covering her with magazines as the flight attendant quickly walked by.

The plane lifted into the sky.

Olivia was a ball of emotions. She had just managed to get through airport security after ferreting from the belly of the Museum the most valuable piece of art to be found in a century or more.

But the next airport would be more unnerving. She would be maneuvering with Egyptian security agents whose language she did not speak. Whose customs she did not know. Whose eyes would not be so easily fooled when they saw the faience.

As she fell into an uncomfortable sleep on Amro's sturdy shoulder, she wondered what would happen if they fell into real trouble ... would he protect her or would she be the pawn?

THIRTY-SEVEN

ometimes the sweetest words are the most
frightening.

She drifted awake to the pilot's voice, "Welcome
to Cairo. We will be landing in just a few minutes."

The rustling of passengers putting their possessions
away and fastening seatbelts filled the plane. Awash with
the saturating North African sun, the plane had taken on
a new ambience. Many of the passengers were speaking
Arabic while the others were tucking away their tourism
brochures or business papers.

She looked up at Amro expecting him to have
snuggled into a cozy sleep with her. Instead he seemed

to have not moved since she fell asleep hours ago. "Did you sleep?"

He nodded that he had not.

"You must be tired?"

"Not at all," he answered matter-of-factly as he placed the dog into the carrier.

"Do I get a good morning?" She asked in her usual cranky morning mood.

"Olivia, this isn't the time for that. We have to honor the ways now of my country."

She wasn't sure if he meant no physical contact or something else. This new mood of his was not comforting.

The possibility that he would use her as a pawn suddenly seemed more likely.

The landing was bumpier than she expected. Amro carefully held the carrier above the plane floor to avoid any damage to the faience. She admired his devotion to the artifact and to returning this art to its rightful place.

But her nerves were getting worse with each minute that went by. She would have given anything to hear Jonathon's calming voice. To talk with him about what she should do next. Trouble was ahead. She felt it. And her intuition was never wrong.

Olivia walked slowly out of the plane. There was nothing else to do but move forward.

Customs waited ahead.

The security agents here seemed different. Less friendly, thinner, more exotic, harder to read. They looked past the other passengers breezing through and observed her with Amro.

Perhaps it was not a good idea for them to have traveled together. She was second-guessing every-thing now.

She looked over at Amro who seemed liked a stranger. He would not even look at her. Still, he seemed completely calm.

As if an instant replay of the St. Louis airport, but in a different backdrop, the faience set alarms off. Olivia wondered if the silly idea of the dog bowl would work here.

These men did not seem so easy to fool. Their penetrating stares seared her skin.

The agent unwrapped the bowl as three others joined him to watch. The faience was revealed. Four agents gasped in unison and spoke fervently in Arabic. Olivia's heart froze.

They knew what this was. Amro said that it had been one of the biggest news stories in Egypt in his lifetime.

Passengers stared. More agents joined and stared at the faience.

In a tone she had never heard from him before, Amro ordered them to do something. She could not understand his Arabic. But the agents came to attention with his order. Two of the agents ran off. The third agent carefully rewrapped the bowl and returned it to the carrier. The other agent looked down at the ground.

They waited.

The next fifteen minutes seemed like hours. Amro leaned back comfortably, checking his Blackberry and enjoying the discomfort of the agents.

Olivia felt trickles of sweat trailing down her back. She was stone quiet. Waiting for whatever he had ordered. The chaos of passengers, luggage, overhead speakers, frayed her nerves. She held on to Amro's composure like a lifeline.

At last the two agents returned with a dignified man in a more elaborate uniform. He took the carrier with the faience in it and ushered them through. Their footsteps clicked in unison as they walked down a hallway toward a row of doors. At the second door, the agents opened it and went inside. The well-dressed man directed them to do the same.

The room, the size of a New York bathroom, was claustrophobic.

Amro and the agents spoke fervently in Arabic. The agents gestured toward the bowl, and then Amro did the same. To her dismay, he then pointed to her.

Her worse fear had come true. He was blaming her for this. Soon she would be taken away to a foreign prison where the U.S. Embassy would have no interest in retrieving her since she had taken the artifact.

The reality of her foolishness sunk in as the agents voices rose to shouts and their gestures became more animated.

The well-dressed man suddenly laughed. Olivia stared at him in shock. Did he think it was funny that this American girl had gotten involved in this international debacle?

He shook his head and seemed to admonish the agents, directing them to leave the room. The door shut behind them. Olivia's heart raced.

He looked at Amro and smiled, patting him on the shoulder.

Completely confused, she looked at Amro and then the well dressed man smiled at her and said in perfect English, "Welcome to Cairo, miss. Please allow me to introduce myself. I'm the head of security here at the Cairo International Airport."

His dark eyes sparkled with delight at her surprise.

"Your travel here," he looked at the faience knowingly, "is much appreciated. Please enjoy Cairo."

Nodding to Amro, he left the room leaving the door open and welcoming them to the freedom of the hallway. The two men put on a good show of laughing about the "mistake" as they walked through the airport. The well-dressed man smiled and waived goodbye as they pushed back the encroaching cab drivers hustling for the business and grabbed the waiting taxi with the open back door.

The driver snaked through the cobweb of tight Cairo streets. Olivia was shell-shocked by the amount of disorganized traffic, continual near collisions and honking horns, throngs of people on the street, and the debris littering the sidewalks. The cab had no air conditioning. The heat seemed to be an entity in itself. Clawing at her body and making her skin prickle from the moisture robbing dryness.

At the same time she was mesmerized by the architecture from another time, unlike anything she had ever experienced, mingled with modern life and a clash of cultural dress and styles. Confusion was not something to be fixed here. It was a natural way of life.

A way of life one would have to understand implicitly to survive in. She wanted to reach out and hold Amro's hand.

"Olivia, we're headed to the market. My uncle is waiting there. I'm sorry, but there is not time for a tour beforehand."

"Of course." As she looked around at the warmth of the old buildings she realized that she wished there was time to explore. Something about this overwhelming city had her mystified. The energy in Cairo was different. Too complex to understand in such a short time. But, regardless of the chaotic streets, the garbage, the gritty façade, something here warmed her heart.

The market was a convergence of old world and new. Brightly colored textiles were displayed amongst fresh fruit, jewelry, rugs, sandals, and touristy pyramid crafts.

"Is there time to walk through the market?"

He laughed. "You smell shopping I see. But no, this is not possible. My uncle is waiting."

She nodded.

"You know who my uncle is?"

"Yes. Dr. Hasaneen."

The cab driver shifted in his front seat, darting a quick look at them in the mirror. She realized her mistake in saying Amro's uncle's name. In this country, Dr. Hasaneen was a national celebrity.

Amro returned to his casual demeanor. Kissing her lightly on the cheek in the privacy of the cab, he rewarded her, "Yes! You're so good."

She smiled coyly. Actually, Jonathon's father's corporate research team was so good. No need to mention that.

"So, in the next block, we'll stop and wait for you to meet him at El Fishawy Café. It's a famous and one of the oldest cafés in Cairo. It's just one block ahead straight ahead."

"You're not coming?"

"No. I thought you might surprise him with our little gift."

She saw that he was observing the listening cab driver. It looked like there was still time for Amro to use her as a pawn. Was someone waiting to take her captive or to take the faience? Maybe he just could not risk being seen with her and the faience in this city where he was well known.

Olivia had never felt so uncomfortable in her life.

There was no way out of this tunnel she had dug for herself. Each step could be leading to her grave, imprisonment, or the most spectacular heist in decades.

The car stopped.

He nodded down the street, "Just one block and you can see the coffee shop with the little outdoor tables? You will recognize him of course. I'll wait inside the cab for you."

Lifting the dog carrier with the faience in it, he handed it to her and popped open her door for her exit. Cleopatra woke suddenly from her sleep and darted out of the cab. Without pause, Olivia scooped her up and slipped her into the back of the carrier. Before the car door closed, she also grabbed her backpack and slipped it over her shoulder. She wasn't taking any chances that he would wait for her here.

Walking the block toward the coffee shop felt like she was walking down the gangplank. She watched every person that passed her. Would they try to grab the dog carrier with the faience in it? Would they try to grab her and toss her in the back of a car? Would they handcuff her and take her to jail? Every face looked suspicious.

Within a few yards of El Fishawy Café's outdoor tables, she scanned the guests looking for Dr. Hasaneen, recalling his face from the broadcast news interviews and newspaper photos. He was a distinguishable man and easy to recognize. Sitting in the center of the outdoor tables, he looked up as she approached the table.

She was out of breath. Not from the short walk. Not from the penetrating heat. Because of the eyes she felt watching her. Someone was watching her every move. And it wasn't Amro or Dr. Hasaneen.

Olivia wanted to run … to plummet through the Cairo streets and far away from this place. All her instincts told her that she was being watched.

"Hello?" Dr. Hasaneen inquired.

There was no turning back now. She had come here to return the faience and, whatever the price, it would be done.

"Dr. Hasaneen?"

"Yes."

"I have a gift to return to you."

"To return?"

"Yes."

With that, she swiftly unzipped the dog carrier keeping her dog securely inside, retrieved the faience, and handed him the wrapped bowl.

"What is this?"

The Café's guests, people walking by, and the waiters watched unabashedly.

Bubble wrap fell from the careful and experienced hands of the Egyptian head of antiquities. The cloth pealed away with his fingertips and sent a roar of Arabic exclamation that Olivia dimly heard as she backed through the flow of people coming closer to Dr. Hasaneen's table to see the most magnificent artifact in the art world. She knew there would only be seconds before they would turn to see her, wonder who she was, and try to stop her.

She turned to run back to Amro's taxi. He was still waiting.

"Olivia!"

Who was calling her name? Amro's taxi door was closed. He was taking no chance of being seen.

From the side street, no wider than an alley, she heard her name again. Almost past the alley, she turned to see a dark limousine. And standing beside it was Jonathon.

Tears poured as she pivoted and ran to Jonathon's car.

In the cool reprieve of the limo, she gave Jonathon the unadorned and complete hug of a child. Streets whizzed by as Olivia curled into his embrace, her back-pack and dog carrier, with Cleopatra tucked snuggly inside, on the floorboard. The limo driver was adept at rocking the car through the side streets to avoid the congestion. She listened, waiting for sirens. "Are we being followed?"

"I don't think so."

"How did you get here? How did you know where would I be? Where did you find this amazing driver?" she gushed.

Jonathon smiled nonchalantly. "Fortunately I have a father with a private jet. And his research team is pretty good."

"Pretty good?"

"Speaking of research…" he handed her his Blackberry. On the screen, she could see the *St. Louis Sun Journal* website linked to the headline news of the day:

Suspect of Museum Murders Arrested

A guard at the Art Museum was arrested today for both murders of the museum's director and board chair. The guard, 38-year-old Brian Brown, had worked at the museum for two years after a termination from his position as a pharmacist for a pharmacy chain. The museum claimed to have no knowledge of the termination or the guard's struggle with schizophrenia.

After the Egyptian artifact was declared missing yesterday, the guard turned himself in to authorities. Brown confessed to using cyanide for both murders. He told police that he believes the artifact has returned to the "mother land."

Brown, an evening graduate student majoring in archeology, told authorities that the Egyptian artifact had talked to him and demanded to be returned to Cairo. He refused to say if he had any part in the artifact gone missing.

Police had Brown on a suspect list after he had told them in an earlier interview that he was angry at the museum for their inappropriate methods in acquiring the artifact and the improper humidity environment of St. Louis that would cause detriment to the piece.

Brown's part-time employee health plan did not include a pharmacy plan.

Olivia looked up into Jonathon's sky blue eyes. She felt ill.

He rubbed her hand. "Don't second guess yourself, Liv."

"I'm confused. What's real and not real? Is the curse real?"

Jonathon sighed, "We may never know. But I do believe Miles' life was in danger. From the curse, from the guard, from the curse's effect on the guard – whichever it was. But the faience is back where it should be. Feel good about that. It's as it should be."

"But it felt so real, Jonathon."

"Maybe it was."

The car stopped abruptly in front of a modern tall building. Jonathon grabbed the carrier with Cleopatra tucked inside and the backpack, helping Olivia out of the car.

"Thanks Ahmed."

"My pleasure, sir."

The sliding doors opened as they entered the cool building and took the elevator to the roof deck. Olivia leaned against the wall of the elevator, still reeling from the newspaper story revelation.

"Liv, it will be ok. We did the right thing."

She knew what he said was true. Had they not involved the guard in the heist, Miles would have been his next target. So it was an intervention of sorts.

The wind of the helicopter blades blasted them as they opened the door to the roof.

Jonathon smiled at her surprise. "Let's go home now after some rest at my father's place in Paris."

"Is it safe to go home?" she shouted over the whir of the helicopter.

"I think they're satisfied that they caught their man."

Seconds later Jonathon, Olivia, and her dog were settled into the helicopter and lifted into the sky.

As they headed north away from the city, Olivia turned to look back. She remembered the feeling of the faience in her hands, the energy she felt when she unwrapped it and saw it for the first time, the reaction it caused when Dr. Hasaneen revealed it at the coffee shop, the way Cairo made her feel…

Looking down toward the market area where she had returned the mystical faience, she muttered, "It felt so real."

A flash of light from the street below shone toward the helicopter like a mirror reflecting in the sun trying to communicate a message. It sparkled like a brilliant star as they drifted away from Cairo.

TUNNELS, CAPPUCCINO, AND A HEIST

MICHELE BONNELL

A READER'S GUIDE

QUESTIONS AND TOPICS FOR DISCUSSION

1. Olivia is passionate about art and artists. Do you think this is the main reason for her involvement in the heist or is it her love for her ex-fiancé Miles?

2. Do you think Jonathon is overshadowed by Miles at the Museum? And with Olivia?

3. Do you believe in repatriation or returning art to the country of origin in cases of the black market or the spoils of war or new regimes?

4. In what way did religious and cultural differences play a role or add tension?

5. What did you think of Omar?

6. Do you think Olivia should have returned from New York City to St. Louis with her then fiance Miles?

7. Did the media act as another character in the novel?

8. How many cultures and countries were in *Tunnels, Cappuccino, And AHeist?*

9. What did you think of the role of the dog?

10. Do you believe in the Egyptian curse and magic?

11. How important is art in our lives and societies?

12. Do you think the museum should have returned the artifact?

13. How did Olivia's Cherokee roots play a role in her passion about repatriation?

ABOUT THE AUTHOR

Michele Bonnell was first featured at the age of eleven in a small town newspaper after receiving a hand-signed letter from the United States President. The journalist asked her if she wanted to be a politician. She replied no, "I want to be writer."

After working in the communications fields for a couple decades, she's wrapping up that media statement by becoming her eleven-year-old vision of a writer – a novelist.

This is her first published novel. She lives in St. Louis with her Papillon Chloe.

CPSIA information can be obtained
at www.ICGtesting.com
Printed in the USA
LVHW112322100619
620807LV00001B/37/P